Of One Blood

Soren Brockdorf

Silent E Publishing Company
4446 Hendricks Ave, #141
Jacksonville, FL 32207

ISBN-10: 0-9755104-5-2

ISBN-13: 978-0-9755104-5-2

1 2 3 4 5 6 7 8 9

1.

Brad Penn studied the heavy, lined face on his television, observed the pale lips as they moved, and noted the film of sweat which glistened on its brow. He was riveted by the words which floated from this talking head, and he wondered if it could possibly be true that their lives – his life, the lives of his wife and two boys, the lives of all of their family, their neighbors, indeed the very "life" they had always known and which they seemed to believe would always be theirs – might just depend on knowing every possible detail uttered by the image on the screen before him, this hollow man.

The Center for Disease Control in Atlanta had just issued another official statement: *Doctors have been unable to control or treat the Negra 9 virus. It has been three months since the President convened a special committee comprised of research scientists as well as officials from the Federal Emergency Management Agency, and the CDC has learned little about this disease. Reports of illness vary widely, but the victims – all female – are believed to number in the thousands, and cases have been reported in nearly all major urban areas. The World Health Organization is considering a moratorium on travel across U.S. borders, and the federal government is urging concerned citizens to stay close to home if possible and to safeguard their homes and communities.*

"We have with us today Dr. Rosenthal," the television news anchor stated. Viewers had always been comforted by Pete Jones, who had brought them through war, who had reported on other catastrophes around the world in a voice which seemed to say, *Not us...we are safe here*, but who now appeared visibly shaken. His voice was weak and nasally.

"Doctor, where are we in our research? What do we know?"

"To be completely honest, Pete, it appears we still know almost nothing about the virus itself. We only know vague details. As you already know, with the first reported case of Negra 9, there were nine black spots on each of the women's ovaries. At this juncture, we neither truly understand how the spots form, nor how they attack the ovaries."

"Do we at least know why there are nine spots?"

"The latest studies suggest that nine seems to be the mode."

"What do you mean by the mode?"

"It is the most common number in the overall structure of the virus."

"What else has been learned?" Pete Jones asked, but his voice carried no trace of hope.

"We have found…" the doctor started to say, and then trailed off. He was clearly defeated. "We have nothing new at this time."

"What are some of the theories out there, Doctor?" Pete asked the physician.

"There are some theories, but I couldn't say any of them are workable yet. We don't even know enough to test them."

Nobody is even angry about this, Brad thought; *they've already moved on to silent abandonment.* Each new hope for an answer, for an antidote, had been quashed. It was the first time he had ever witnessed such utter resignation, such hopelessness. The doctor continued, "The virus is not destroying the ovaries. It is somehow taking them over and shutting them down, as it were. It is stopping them from performing their normal function."

Pete asked, "What are you saying, Doctor?"

What now? Brad wondered. *How could things get any worse?* All that was left to do was to try and lead as normal a life as possible.

"At this point we can't tell exactly what it is doing to the ovaries. All we know for sure is it's stopping the ovaries' ability to produce eggs."

"Why would it want to do this?"

"Want? Viruses are different from bacteria, certainly, but they still don't *want* to do anything. They have no will. They do not have the ability to willfully take control of other life forms."

Pete blinked at the camera. A thick silence seeped from the TV, dead air.

"We just don't know much yet," the doctor finally said.

"How long is it going to take to figure it out, Doctor?"

The doctor fidgeted awkwardly, and now a droplet of sweat ran down and off the end of his nose. "We have no answers at this time."

"Are you saying, in your opinion, we will not be able to stop this?"

"Frankly, I have no idea how we can. Right now we have every single scientist with any expertise in viral research working on this problem. At the rate this disease is spreading, within three months, millions of women across the country will have completely lost the ability to reproduce."

"In your view, then, the outlook is quite grim?"

"Look. I know it sounds like the proverbial doomsday projection, but without a significant breakthrough very soon, we may reach a point where we will see a sharp decrease in the birth rate for the United States. An alarming decrease, I would say."

The man on the news sat there, again unable to say anything, the old familiar confidence, the comforting glance up at the camera, all gone.

Brad thought, *No further population growth. They're saying we could be the last generation? It's like a big joke, isn't it? For so long, everyone ran around worrying about overpopulation... Now look at us.* And then a thought: *Maybe it is a joke, after all. Maybe it's all a huge hoax!* He had not seen any real victims with his own eyes. But no, the graveness of the faces on the screen

– and something in his own gut – told him that there was truth in this. Just how much truth was hard to say.

"Let's turn now to Dr. McLaughlin. Doctor, you have two areas of expertise, one in actuarial science, and the other in statistics. What is our probability of success?"

This talking head was thin and bony, with round glasses in metallic frames perched upon it. "We're not optimistic at the present moment," the skull said.

"That's not a very scientific answer. Statistically speaking, what are our chances of finding a cure or at least a vaccine for this virus?"

"I can give you all the information you want. I could tell you about R-squares, P-tests, and coefficients, but statistically speaking, we don't have much chance, as things stand now."

"Doctor, what are we facing statistically?" Pete asked.

"We're looking at close to a million to one for the foreseeable future, given our current lack of progress."

A million to one, Brad thought. *The old cliché is finally made real.*

Pete tried to smile. "After speaking to you two, I think we're going to have to find some new guests."

Dr. Rosenthal sat there, grim-faced, but oddly, the other one, the skeletal McLaughlin, chuckled in a strange, clotted way.

Brad Penn stared at the skull, unnerved and entranced at the same time. Then, from the other room, he heard the voices of his children, his two boys: Alex, eight, and Ben, who had just turned six. He instinctively shut off the TV so as to not alarm the little ones. He could hear them come screaming around the corner like NASCAR drivers.

Car number-eight raced past car six through the doorway, engine roaring. Both slammed into the finish line – Dad – who was leaning back against the couch. There was a huge pile-up on the track: two cars and a dad spilled out on the tarmac. Then, the make-believe race suddenly forgotten, Alex yelled,

"Daddy, Daddy, let's shoot some hoops! Come on!"

Both boys were hopping up and down madly. Brad stared at them. His mind felt frozen and faraway. A moment of horror filled him – it was as if he could not recall their names, did not even know them. When he took Alex's wiry forearm in his hand, he came to himself once again. "Okay," he said. "You guys go find the ball. I'll be there in a minute."

The two cars sprang to life again, always in fourth gear, and they thundered out of the room.

Sarah Penn, Brad's wife, came in quietly and sat on the sofa next to her husband. He could not look at her.

"I heard it on the set in the kitchen," she said. It was the same tone she used late that night when Ben had been sick with pneumonia at age two and again when she called him at work to tell him that Alex had broken his arm on the playground, her forced-calm, emergency-room voice.

"What do you think is happening?"

"I don't know," he said. "I never imagined something like this was possible. It's like a movie."

Brad looked up at her. She had borne his children, weathered the storm of his being fired from his first job selling insurance, nursed him through the death of his father, dealt with two miscarriages and a C-section, and she was still beautiful. What was it in her face that still got to him in the same way? It wasn't sexiness, it was…strength. Finally, he felt he knew the word. Strength and those brown eyes.

Sarah felt somewhat lost inside herself. It wasn't just the disastrous news. For years now she had felt frustrated, afraid she would grow old and never have known her place on this earth. Vaguely, she had always known she wanted to help people, but wasn't sure how she should begin. It was too late for her to go back to school, and besides, she was never good enough in her science classes to even consider medical school (this was a great source of humor in her family, since her father had been a highly regarded geologist). She had often done charitable work around Lake City, but she secretly aspired to something greater – one of those trips to Haiti or the Dominican Republic, to help the children there, but again, she wasn't sure where to plunge in. And anyway, the two boys were her life, mostly. *Funny,* she thought, *how you think the diapers and the bottles will never end, and you complain about it, and you swear you're done, and then you wake up one day longing for the smell of a baby. You look at your big boys, and you wish they were little again.* But, in fact, they *were* done. Brad had agreed to go in for a vasectomy this coming fall, and in the meantime she would remain on the pill. Now she could only watch the boys grow and feel them moving away from her day by day, nobody ever pausing long enough just to say, Wait a minute…can't we just all slow down a bit?!

"We can't have anymore now," Brad said.

She was startled. "What?"

"We can't have the TV on when the kids are around. Don't want anymore bad news right now."

"Oh, I know," she said. "What's going to happen to this old world?"

Brad shook his head. Slowly he stood up and moved towards the front door. He stopped for a moment and gazed back at her. *Strength*, he thought. That's the word. He walked out into the bright sunlight to play with the boys.

"You have to dribble it," he said to the Ben. "You can't hold it and run around. You have to dribble it. Try to dribble it. No, don't slap it, push it."

Ben slapped the ball and it bounced lower and lower, until finally it came to rest between the concrete and the boy's hand. He picked it up, and tried again.

Alex said, "That's double dribbling! You can't do that!"

Ben picked up the ball and threw it at his brother, exasperated. "I can't dribble!"

Brad loved playing ball with his boys, but he saw already that sports would not come naturally to them, as they had to him. But that was all right. His job was a nine-to-five no-brainer, peddling insurance, but it paid the bills and he had time to coach some little league, and every Saturday was a picnic at the ballpark, and everyone had fun and that was all that mattered. Someday he would be driving them to high-school practices or maybe play rehearsals or science fairs or something, and they would have their little moments of glory and all would be well. This was America – you could never run out of options.

Alex did about the same as Ben had done, slapping at the ball instead of pushing it, but at least it bounced steadily so he could move towards the basket. He picked up the ball and shot it.

It clanged off the rim, and Ben grabbed it up again. "Betcha can't get it from me, Dad," he said, smiling.

"Bet I can." Brad lifted his arms in the air, and Ben froze and laughed. He tried unsuccessfully to dribble again. He tucked the ball under his arm, ran to the basket, and threw one up awkwardly. To everyone's amazement, it dropped through the net, a perfect swish. Alex fell down on the driveway laughing. Brad leaned over and put his hands on his knees.

His kids, his yard. His home. But now the hopelessness swarmed at him again. Maybe here with his kids he could hold it together. Things seemed pretty normal – nowhere near the sort of war zone you saw in news clips from Iraq and places like that. Whenever he ventured out, all seemed calm. People were still buying groceries and going to work. He was here in his yard, playing ball with his kids. He watched Alex rolling over and over, in the grass now. Ben still had his arms raised in triumph and amazement. His dark hair picked up the sunlight.

I mean, how bad can it really be? Brad thought.

2

Dr. Maria Escobar watched her husband Tomas as he placed his hands on the other woman. He was forty now, but he exhibited the ease and grace of a younger man, standing perfectly still and cupping her backbone with his palm, as in turn she draped her arm in a crescent across his shoulders. Their bodies began to move, their bare thighs touching.

She knew it was a necessary part of Tomas's work – he made his living as a professional ballroom dancer – but she hated seeing him with this blonde twenty-something. Maria herself was thirty-four, and in very good shape, too…quite lovely, in fact, but she could not help noticing the way Tomas stared back into his partner's half-closed eyes. He never looked at *her* that way anymore.

She leaned back on her chaise lounge, drinking her bourbon-laced Fazenda Cachoeira coffee, watching the two of them as they swirled about the turquoise swimming pool. It was a Saturday, a casual rehearsal for an upcoming competition, and the late-afternoon Spanish sun lit them in a cinematic aura. They wore swimsuits, and of all the men she had known in Valencia and beyond, Tomas was still the most handsome, with a large, friendly face, a thick mustache, and bronzed skin. It had always been difficult to go out to dinner with him, he attracted so much attention from other girls, but she had simply gotten used to it. He was strong, hard, and gallant, a man who was meant to be loved by many women, and she accepted this, for she felt that he loved her only. Still, she tried not to cater too much to his little needs and wishes, as he could be a difficult man to live with, but she thought this was probably true of most men. She had seldom known anyone more strong-willed than Tomas. His career had been completely self-made through his talent and determination, although his career was now waning, just as her own (she was a professor of paleontology) was reaching its pinnacle. She had to agree that he was still something to look at even though one could tell that under his chin and around his waist things were not as tight as they had once been. But put the man in a white shirt and black slacks, and he might still pass for twenty-five.

Sometimes she wondered again what difference children might have made in their marriage. They had never had children. They had discussed it only once, years before, and had agreed that their careers were too important to them. The subject had never come up again, though she thought of it secretly from time to time.

She kept another secret as well. It was in her lap at the moment. She had begun reading the Bible again, the little red pocket paperback her mother had slipped to her a few days before she had died, two years ago. She had it tucked into a fashion magazine – not because she thought Tomas would disapprove, but because reading it was to her something all her own, something untouched by his strong will. As a girl, she had gone regularly to Mass with her mother and father, and she had read it in its entirety several times, in Spanish, but this one was in English. At one time, on a strange whim, she had started a collection of Bibles in various languages, sometimes stealing them from hotels or libraries.

She thumbed back to the book of *Genesis*, to the passage where Abraham is first mentioned. She liked that part, especially.

She glanced up and saw that Tomas was winding up his practice session. At that instant, he drew the young blond girl close to him and kissed her. For a brief second, she thought that their lips lingered a bit too long, but then she thought, *No, no, that's just Tomas, that is how he is. Just a goodbye kiss. Don't be jealous. Say nothing.*

When the girl had gone, he came strolling over to her, and smiled.

"Productive session?" she asked.

"Yes, fine." He reached over to the patio table and picked up the small, steel-stringed guitar he had bought for himself two months ago, and sat beside her on the chaise.

"Do you really think you will be able to play that thing?" Maria asked.

"Absolutely," he replied. "I'm starting my second career as a classical guitarist."

It had gotten more difficult lately for her to tell when he was joking. He was smiling, but his tone was quite serious.

"Maybe you should at least buy a real classical guitar," she said. "Once you retire from your present career, that is."

"I can never retire. My fans adore me too much."

She smiled at him and said nothing. She worried about him sometimes.

He stood up, put the guitar back on the table, took a CD out of its case, and put it in the little stereo. "One day I will play just like this. Just like Joaquin Rodrigo."

"I hope you will. I mean, certainly you will."
There was no point in raining on his optimism.

"I'll play like this one day," he said again, and the first strains of Rodrigo's *Junto Al Generalife* fluttered from the player.

They sat there listening; it was soothing there in the bright sun, with the sound of the guitar. Next was Angel Romero playing the guitar in a much more rhythmic style. She stood up, pulled Tomas toward her and said, "Why don't you ever dance with *me*?"

He said nothing, but smiled and took her hand, and stood up. They moved lightly around the floor, her hair twirling, floating through the air. She knew, of course, that she was not as fluid as he – had never been – but this was overshadowed by the joy of the moment.

But he became increasingly more intense. She struggled to keep up with him – even after his exhaustive practice session, he seemed barely to breathe. Ultimately, as the guitar reached its climax, she could not keep up any longer. He whirled her around violently, then at a hard strum of the guitar, he flung her abruptly onto the couch. She fell back; at first anger bit at her, but then all at once she found herself laughing. He sat down next to her, and looked at her. He picked up his guitar again and carefully formed a chord.

"You'll probably never get to play it in public, you know."

"I will play in public." He looked at his fingers.

"You're too serious," she said. Can't you do anything for fun? Can't you just play the guitar for *me*?"

"One day I'll be the best in the world at guitar," he remarked. "When my fingers stop hurting."

"Fine, but I'll insist on traveling with you," she said. "You can point to me in the audience at every concert, and say, 'Ladies and gentlemen, I'd like to introduce my wife, Maria, to whom I owe everything.'" *Of course*, she thought, *all the other women will be there, too. It would be quite a little procession.*

He stood up and looked across the patio at his reflection in the glass door. "Do you think I'm getting fat?" he asked.

She laughed. "I thought *I* was supposed to ask *you* that question."

"No, seriously, I can't stick out too far in the back. I must be like one thin line."

She stood up and opened a new CD, Edward Grieg. She put in *Peer Gynt: Suite Number 1.* She moved silently across the room, placed her hands on his shoulders and kissed him gently on his cheek. They began to sway softly.

But soon the rolling music of the afternoon surrounded them, building in intensity; it had rolled in softly at first, and then it came hard. It came hard again, repeating horns blasting intermittently. They collapsed on the chaise lounge together, not moving as they suffered together through the throes of Ase's death.

Tomas had fallen asleep, his hundred-and-ninety–pound weight on top of her. With a roll of her eyes, she gently slid to one side, but she was trapped. She could just reach her magazine, with the little red Bible inside of it. She grasped it and opened it to the part about Abraham again, and began to read.

She felt that she really loved her life. She loved Valencia. She loved her husband, and she loved her house. It was a square house with a pink clay roof and many different kinds of windows: rectangular, circular, square, but most of them small. All the windows had decorative headers that held flowerpots with vines coming out of them. Attached to the house were iron light fixtures, and iron poles supported green canopies over the windows. Around the front entrance was a marvelous coping, out of which she could gaze and see the guest quarters, and the pool house that matched the house in every detail. The courtyard was bounded by a row of perfectly cut shrubs. An iron fence surrounded the shrubs. *Yes*, she thought, *I have a beautiful home, and a beautiful man.* The only thing that could improve her situation right now would be if she could reach her Neuchatel chocolates across the room. She should wake up his lazy self – how long could she be expected to lie there without her chocolates?

She drifted off again, with Abraham resting on her breast.

"What's that you're reading?" Tomas was standing beside the chaise lounge, rubbing his eyes.

Caught off guard, she had no choice but to tell him the truth. "The Bible," she said. "In English."

"Any good?"

"I'm still on the first part. It certainly starts off with a bang."

"Do you think humankind will be able to provide what God demands?" Tomas asked.

"I don't know," she said. "Abraham's faith was great enough that he would actually have sacrificed his own son."

"It sure was. If I had a son, I certainly wouldn't sacrifice him."

"If *we* had a son, I couldn't imagine doing that."

"You would have to have faith stronger than steel. I don't know where to find that kind of faith."

"Perhaps we need to be blessed and to 'make our descendents as numerous as the stars in the sky and the sand on the seashore,' like it says in here." she said.

"We *are* blessed," he said.

"God helps the needy," she said.

"Let's hope he helps the rising middle class, too."

"Not funny," she said. His smile vanished and he shrugged his shoulders and walked away toward the house.

It really was not funny, Maria thought. She had been following the news reports out of the United States – the virus. What would people do if it began to spread? Would people stick together, or would they fall apart? *The whole world might have to stick together, out of need*, she thought. *We are the needy. God helps the needy. God, help...*

"What are you reading now?" He held a tall, glistening glass in his hand this time. She held up her Bible.

"Still?" he said. "Has the action picked up at all?"

She began to read: " 'When Abraham came to Egypt, the Egyptians saw that Sarah was a beautiful woman.'"

"Aah," he said gently, "no wonder. It's a story about you."

"Yes," she said. "I am married to a seventy-five-year-old man."

"Hmph." He traipsed off once again.

She continued reading about how Abraham and Sarah went to Egypt to look for food when the rest of the land was dry, because the Nile River still had water for crops. Abraham was worried that they would kill him and take his beautiful wife, so he said that Sarah was his sister. Pharaoh took Sarah as his concubine and Abraham received many things because of this. God saw how awful and wicked this was, and he punished Egypt. Pharaoh then ordered Sarah and Abraham to go away again.

"What is Abraham up to?" Tomas asked. He had appeared at the foot of the chaise lounge with a box of ice cream and a spoon.

"He just allowed the Pharaoh to take his wife as a mistress."

"What kind of man would allow that?"

"Not such a great guy," she responded.

"No, not such a great guy. But why would God make a covenant with him when he was not a great guy?"

"The covenant? I thought you hadn't read the Bible."

"I know the gist of it." Tomas spooned ice cream onto his tongue.

"Well, I think it doesn't have anything to do with how great you are. It has to do with accepting what God decides on. If perfection were the standard, God would never accept anyone."

"She must have been quite a wife."

"You haven't even heard the good part. Sarah tells him he can sleep with the maid."

"Wow. Perhaps *we* should get a maid."

"She didn't do it for his pleasure, though," Maria said. "It was a terrible disgrace to them not to have any children. She told Abraham that he could sleep with Hagar so they could bring a child into the world. But then, Sarah became jealous."

"What else would you expect?"

She read: "'The angel of the Lord said to Hagar, you are now with child and you will have a son; you shall name him Ishmael because the Lord has heard of your misery. He will be a wild donkey of a man. His hand will be against everyone and everyone's hand against him and he will live in hostility towards all of his brothers.'"

"That's powerful stuff," Tomas said. "A wild donkey of a man."

"An ass, you might say," she said. "Probably a wonderful dancer, though."

He pretended to ignore this last. He went over and picked up his guitar, looked down at the fret board, and started tuning his A-string exactly where he wanted it. He liked the string tuned a little sharp. He started playing a simple scale, going diagonally across the fret board.

"There you go, playing the devil's music again."

"Ah yes," he said smoothly, "*Diabolus in Musica.*" He smiled and continued playing. The flat fifth was in the exact middle of the scale – Tomas did not know this, really, but he enjoyed the ominous sound it made, and he played it again. He said quite seriously, "I could have been killed for playing this music a few hundred years ago."

She struggled with her temptation to make the obvious sarcastic remark, but fortunately Tomas looked up at her with his little-boy look, and they both broke into laughter at once.

"Yes," she said, "I'm glad you're free from your sins, and allowed to play such music."

"I just want to play jazz," he responded, abruptly serious once again.

"I thought you were determined to play classical."

"Jazz *is* classical," he said. He fumbled around on the neck some more, and then said, "Abraham cracks me up."

"Why?"

"He tried to bargain with God. You can't bargain with God."

"When did he do that?" she asked.

"When God was going to destroy everyone, first he asked Him if He would sweep away the city if there were fifty righteous people. When God said yes, he bargains it down to forty, and then ten."

"He wasn't exactly bargaining," she replied. "In a sense he was, but Abraham was earnestly trying to save the people."

"Salvation? Then why would he offer his daughters to be gang-raped?"

"You have to remember the times," Maria argued. "Women were no more than property back then, to be offered the way you might offer someone...ice cream."

"That will have to remain one of life's mysteries, I suppose," he said. "Kind of like the mystery of the missing harmonics on the guitar."

"What harmonics?"

"Listen." He played through all the natural harmonics. "You see? I can't play a sharp note. They're missing." He went up and down on the frets. "There is no sharp harmonic anywhere, you can't find one."

"I wasn't really looking for one," she said.

She was glad that his newfound love of guitar was clearly entertaining to him. She found it less than interesting, but she felt she had to show some amusement.

She read aloud some more, half to herself: "My Lord, he said, please turn aside to your servant's house; you can wash your feet and spend the night and then go on your way early in the morning." She paused and looked out at the square across the street behind their lot. "Can you imagine back then? They didn't have inns or hotels. When traveling, you entered a city and went to the square. In the square, you would wait for someone to take you to his house to spend the night. That must have required a great deal of trust."

"Or madness," Tomas said.

"Back then you had to have children," she said.

"Why?"

"Children helped you establish power and continuity. That was why Abraham's two daughters got him drunk – they were desperate enough to lie with him and have children."

"I guess they thought birth defects were also the will of God."

"It was just so awful not to have children. Nowadays, some people deliberately try *not* to have children.

"Like us, you mean." He was still looking down at his guitar.

"We never wanted children, I guess." She tried to imagine Tomas holding a baby, but the image would not form in her mind.

"We have our work," he said.

Maria thought about her own mother. All religions teach us to respect the wisdom of aged citizens: they have an honored place in the world. Maria still felt like a little child herself sometimes. Her mother had given her so much. Even if she had ever had a child of her own, had she really anything worthwhile to give? Regret welled up in her for a moment, and then she thought, *It's just that bit of bourbon I put in the iced coffee making me think this way. Or maybe it's the news about the virus in America. It's really all quite disturbing.* She wondered whether Tomas had been following the story. *No. Too concerned with his dance competition.*

"People are strange," he said. "Why would Abraham take such an old woman as a wife?"

She replied, "There were many reasons. Abraham was turning into a great man at that time. People took wives for different reasons. It was not always for endless companionship; sometimes it was for a treaty, or sometimes for a solution." She was surprised by her own sense of authority on the subject. She was a paleontologist, after all, not a sociologist.

"Still, it's a little weird. There had to be a younger woman somewhere whom he could have taken, who would have fulfilled the same requirement."

Tomas stood up again. He never could spend too much time on a subject that did not have to do directly with himself. "One requirement in being a dancer is you must always have a mirror handy." He gazed at his reflection in the glass door and began flexing his muscles.

She looked at him and shook her head. "You know, you really have an ego the size of an elephant."

He smiled, looking at himself, and said absent-mindedly. "I like elephants."

She went back to her book. *'The Lord had closed up every womb in Abimelech's household because of Abraham's wife Sarah.'* *How strangely appropriate*, she thought. *'For the Lord had closed up every womb in Abimelech's household because of Abraham's wife Sarah.'* *Hmm. Maybe the Lord will close up my womb. Maybe that is what is happening with that unthinkable virus in the United States.*

Tomas was still studying his reflection. She asked him, "Have you followed the news from the U.S.? The virus? It's on all the TV stations, in the papers…"

"Yes," he said, turning back to her at last. "I've followed it with a great deal of interest. Do you think God is punishing Americans for the way they live?"

She hesitated. She had not expected that from him. Tomas had never been one to judge others too harshly – he was at least aware of his own extravagances. "Punishing Americans?"

"Sure," he said. "Or perhaps just punishing sinners generally. Do you think this is all the work of God?"

"No," she said. "God does not do evil, but sometimes he lets evil things happen."

"Ah, well, I see that your theology is faulty. Your Old Testament God was very keen to punish. I suggest you give up your studies, maybe buy a dog instead."

"I guess there is always faith."

"Dogs are very faithful."

"No. I mean my own faith that someday I'll understand what's in this book."

"Of course there is faith," he responded, "but you need to have patience and hope."

"I'll be patient as I try to find faith," she said.

"You need to find hope, too. Don't forget hope. Without hope, patience, and faith, we'll never get anyplace."

She looked at him with a new sort of regard. She could not recall ever having talked with him before about such things. Perhaps he really could think more deeply than she suspected.

"In fact," Tomas said, "Hope would be a very good name for a dog, don't you agree?"

She made a face at him. " ' Become righteous in the eyes of the Lord,'" she said.

He brought his silly, handsome face down to hers and kissed her lips, and she kissed back. Even if he was a silly, shallow, beautiful, professional egomaniac, he was her husband, after all, and she was glad.

3

It seemed the whole world had gone crazy, but Mae Ling remained detached from the ordeal while she attempted to eat her tea melon. She was a young woman of twenty-four, living in a world that only recognized men, and which certainly did not approve of deprived, destitute, and abandoned girls. Her life would remain unchanged even though the world was in chaos, because she had always been in chaos.

"Always" was a funny word. "Always" did not describe time as well as it described life. Mae Ling would have been able to go through life pretending that hers was not such a sad existence, but there was always a mirror somewhere to remind her of what she was. She might have been able to move on, but there was always some new sorrow coming towards her. She sustained a meager faith that one day her circumstances would change for the better. In fact, her candle was burning a bit brighter as of late – or perhaps it only looked that way, because so many other candles were burning out. And when she thought of it in this way, a new guilt began gnawing at her.

Her troubles had begun ten years earlier when, at the age of fourteen, she had helped lead an expedition deep into China. *"Lead" is another funny English word*, she thought. Normally one might assume that a leader is in control, gains a certain prestige, but in fact, she had not been much more than a pack mule and interpreter, chosen because her English was quite good. Even though some of the party were from Spain, all had been fluent in English, and so that had been their common language on the journey.

Jining was a city of a hundred and eighty thousand people in an autonomous inner Mongolian region of China. It was an important railroad junction, connecting Beijing and Lanzhou, and the Republics of Mongolia and Russia. The expeditionary party had come by train and spent the three days getting ready. Mae Ling met them at their hotel the morning they were to leave for the expedition to the Gobi Desert.

There had been no formal introduction, just an expectation of service. She was waiting in the lobby as the party came down. The first to arrive were Tomas Escobar and his wife, Dr. Maria Escobar, a paleontologist, although at the time, Mae Ling had not really been certain what that meant.

"You must be our guide," Tomas said.

"Yes, thank you. How do you like our city so far?" Mae Ling asked.

"I hate it, to be quite honest."

She overheard Maria's sharp whisper: "Tomas, this is her home."

"I don't care if it's her home," he said, quite loudly. "This place is miserable. They say not to drink the water. I say the food is disgusting. Our waitress last night was probably the stupidest woman on the planet. I told her to make me a vodka on the rocks. She did not even know how to put ice in a glass of vodka."

"Maybe she didn't understand you," Maria offered.

"Vodka and ice? We're right next door to Russia. How difficult could it be?"

"Tomas, you need to calm down."

"They say this place is known for meat packing. I can't imagine anyone eating the meat from this place. The only real exports they have here are tetanus, botulism, and salmonella."

"Tomas..." Maria said again.

"It's okay," Mae Ling said. "Many people from Europe find it hard to get accustomed to this place."

"This is the most backwards city I've ever been in."

"Maybe you will like the countryside better," Mae Ling suggested.

"I can't possibly like it any less," Tomas said.

"That's enough out of you," Maria said.

She was appalled by her husband's behavior, but in part she blamed herself. This trip could be crucial to her career and reputation, and she saw that she had made an error in bringing him along – he was too temperamental, too self-absorbed, to take part in such a journey.

Another scientist, Dr. John Pippins, from America, and his daughter Sarah came down the stairway entrance. Sarah was not much older than Mae Ling, perhaps around eighteen, but she carried herself like the other adults.

"Good morning, Dr. Pippins, " Maria said. "And good morning to you, Sarah."

"Hello, Dr. Escobar! How has your stay been so far?" Pippins asked.

"Oh, very nice, very nice," she replied. Her stern glance at Tomas kept him quiet for the moment.

Pippins turned to their guide. "Mae Ling, I saw the funniest thing last night."

"What was that?"

"I saw a man on a little three-wheeled bike. I think it was his version of a motor home. I couldn't believe all the things he had loaded on that bike. He had everything one could imagine – a sofa and a lounge chair. He was a little guy, too. And he wore a baseball cap, argyle sweater, dress pants, and dress shoes, but he was pedaling down the road like nothing bothered him."

"Yes, that's how some people live here," Mae Ling said.

"Well, that's not a bad way," said John. "Makes us Americans look ridiculous with our huge cars and expensive homes. And all the bills that go along with them."

Maria was beginning to admire John's outlook on life. He seemed to understand people from different places and he was entertained by it all – able to absorb whatever the world had to offer. He seemed quite at peace with himself.

"So what did you eat last night?" asked Mae Ling.

"I have no idea," John said. "The menu was a mystery to me. I wish you had been there."

Mae Ling shone under his gaze. He managed to make her feel important.

"We have mostly eaten at a market outside a building on a street I can't name," he said with a smile. "I'm not exactly sure what I ate there either, but I enjoyed the lady who sold the meal to us. Very nice lady in a red blouse."

"Oh, yes," Maria said. "I know the woman you mean. I bought something from her yesterday." Maria's heart had gone out to the woman in the market. She stood there all day, every day, selling food. However, she was pleasant, and did her job well, and that was all that seemed to matter to her. She looked happy with her tied-up blouse, tied-up hair, and khaki pants. All the women seemed to like pigtails or short hair. They looked comfortable in their flats, loose blouses and baggy pants.

John said, "If you gave a man a scooter in this town, he could just about do anything. If you tried to start a business in the United States for a million dollars, you could barely attract attention." He pointed across the street. "I wonder what you call that thing." The object was half-bike, half-car. It had headlamps, a canvas top, and sides.

Sarah chipped in, "I think he calls it home."

When all the bags had been brought down, Mae Ling started putting them in the truck out front. They all piled into the truck, and Dr. Pippins, who had been elected to do the driving, turned around to make sure all was okay.

"I guess we're off," he said.

Tomas spoke mockingly. "What joy."

Maria was starting to have enough of him. "Tomas, this might be one of the most exciting experiences we will ever have," she said. "Why can't you try for five minutes to appreciate it?"

Tomas ignored her and spoke to Pippins. "So, where is this place, John?"

Pippins turned to him effusively. "It will be quite exciting, very exciting. Geologically speaking, it's incredible. We'll be near the desert basin in the Altai Mountains, the grasslands and Steppes of Mongolia, with the Tibetan plateau to the north, and the North China Plain to the southwest."

"What does Gobi' mean?" Sarah asked.

"Gobi just means 'desert' in Mongolian," her dad responded.

"But I thought you were a planetary geologist," Tomas said.

"I am. Planetary geology means you study a smaller subset of geology, but all of geology is exciting."

"Hmm. How big is this place?" Tomas asked. Maria was grateful for his sudden interest – maybe he was trying after all.

"Well, the Gobi measures about sixteen hundred kilometers from southwest to northeast, and eight hundred kilometers from north to south. It occupies one million, three hundred thousand square miles, one of the largest deserts in the world."

"Great," Tomas said. "I look forward to having sand in my shoes all day."

"No, no," John said. "Quite the contrary. This desert is not sandy. It's covered by bare rock." Tomas looked out the window.

"A geologist's dream," said Maria.

"Yes, but a paleontologist's dream, too," Pippins said.

"That's true." Maria smiled.

"A dancer's nightmare," Tomas said. "One large, hot, flat rock."

John turned. "Perhaps you should take up meteorology, then. It is a meteorologist's dream as well. The Gobi has great extremes and rapidly changing weather, and not just throughout the year, but every day. It can change by as much as thirty-two degrees centigrade in one day."

"That's huge," Sarah said.

"Yes, it is. It can even get to fifty degrees centigrade in parts of the Gobi while there are icy sandstorms and snowstorms in spring and early summer. There is a run here called the Hellish Race because participants have to run it over the course of six days, carrying heavy bags containing food and drinks."

"Intriguing," Tomas said.

Maria turned to Sarah. "What's really exciting about the Gobi is it has the most incredible fossil finds in history. They even found the first dinosaur egg here."

"Wow!" Sarah said. "Do you think we'll find a dinosaur egg?"

"Even better," Maria said, "we're going to find a meteorite that actually struck a dinosaur; it's the only spot in the world where the remains of a meteor are sitting right on top of fossilized dinosaur bones."

"Wow!" Sarah said again.

Mae Ling said, "And if you like animals, Sarah, you should look for the black-tailed gazelles, and sand plovers.

If you like birds and fauna, you'll find sparrows, saltwart, gray sagebrush, and low grasses."

"Mae Ling?"

"Yes, Sarah."

"What about lunch?"

Mae Ling smiled. "Well, for lunch we have the sandwiches prepared by the hotel. But tonight, I will cook for you all. It will be something you'll really like."

"You promise?"

"I'll do my best."

Tomas looked at her coldly. "What is your role in this expedition, Sarah?" he asked.

She hesitated for a moment and then said, "I'm writing a paper for my freshman composition class."

"Ah. And what is your thesis?" Tomas said.

"It's very interesting. My title is 'Did it Take Place? An Investigation into the Travels of Marco Polo'," she said proudly. "My dad helped me with the title."

"Interesting. Tell me more," Tomas said, looking out the window.

"There's a huge debate about how much of Marco Polo's exploits were true, and how much was false. On Marco Polo's deathbed, a priest begged him to confess that it was mostly lies, but he insisted that 'I've not told half of what I saw!'"

"Well, what are the facts?" Maria asked.

"The skeptics say that in all his writings he never mentioned Chinese writing, chopsticks, tea, and, if you can believe it, the dude never mentioned the Great Wall."

"Very curious," Tomas said.

"Yes, but he does go into detail about paper money, the Grand Canal, and the Mongol army. He talks about tigers, the Imperial Postal System, and he writes about Japan, which he refers to by its Chinese name, Zipang. It was the first time western literature ever mentioned Japan."

"What do you think your answer to the question will be?"

"I don't know," Sarah said. "I hope to get a feel for the land, and maybe come up with my own opinion, whatever it might be. No matter what the answer is, from what I've read so far, he was definitely one of the world's greatest storytellers." Her sincerity on the subject was quite clear to them all. Sarah could conceive that anyone might *not* be interested in the life of Marco Polo. He had spent seventeen years in China and India. Just to be here was a marvel. In fact, in 1266, he had been right where she was now. He had been in Khanbaliq, now Beijing.

"Why did he come to Mongolia?" Maria asked.

"Kubla Khan asked Pope Gregory the Tenth to bring educated people to Mongolia," Sarah said. "Marco Polo was sent because he was a great linguist. He knew four languages and was a favorite of the Khan."

"Well, that all sounds fascinating," Maria said. "I hope your essay goes well."

Sarah beamed. She felt as though she were a member of the party, almost an equal among these highly educated people. She was utterly happy. "I do too, but if I don't, I still have an ending."

"How's that?" Maria asked.

"I'm going to end it with a quote from the book Marco Polo wrote: 'I believe it was God's will that we should come back so that men might know the things that are in the world, since, as we have said in the first chapter of this book, no other man, Christian or Saracen, Mongol or Pagan, has explored so much of the world as Messer Marco, son of Messer Niccolo Polo, great and noble citizen of the City of Venice.' If you believe all his books, he sure did travel a long ways. Although many of those miles were by ship, he covered a lot of ground. But I guess I'm talking too much."

"Not at all," Maria said.

"Anyway, tell me about the dinosaur we're going to see, and the meteor."

"We are going to look at a Tsintaosaurus."

"What does that mean?" Sarah asked.

"The dinosaur is named after the region in Northern China where the first one was found."

"How big were they?"

"About nine meters long," Maria answered.

"Hmm, let's see. That would be…" Sarah asked.

"About thirty feet," Mae Ling broke in

"That's correct," said Maria.

"What did they eat?" Sarah asked. She had her father's sense of inquiry.

"It was a plant eater. It was a duck-billed dinosaur, or what we would call a hadrosaur. It had a very bizarre head decoration – a head spike sticking up from its forehead, kind of like a unicorn."

"Yes," Sarah said excitedly.

Mae Ling spoke up again. "Westerners originally thought the Chinese put that spike there so that they would get credit for discovering a new dinosaur, but everyone now knows that it was real."

"That's right, Mae Ling," Maria said. "You know a little about dinosaurs, don't you?"

"Yes," she said softly. Or maybe she knew a great deal. Why would Maria assume she only knew a little?

"The Gobi Desert has a wealth of fossils from animals not found in North America. A man named Roy Chapman Andrews and his team came to the desert back in the 1920s and found the first nest of dinosaur's eggs. The eggs were from a Protoceratops," Maria said.

"When did they live?" Sarah asked.

"This particular dinosaur lived in the late Cretaceous period. We had the Triassic, the Jurassic, and then the Cretaceous."

Sarah nodded. She may not have known much about dinosaurs, but from her father, she certainly knew her time periods.

Maria went on: "Our dinosaur was in the late Cretaceous, which meant he was one of the last dinosaurs to roam the earth. There was a great flood about a hundred million years ago, about in the middle of the Cretaceous period, and it went away. The seas receded and the lands that were once separated were connected again, and the dinosaurs could roam the world. But that's not what killed our dinosaur," said Maria.

"No," Sarah's father said. "Our dinosaur was killed by a meteorite."

"Now that's some bad luck. What exactly is a meteorite? I mean, I know it's like a big rock…"

"The word meteor comes from the Greek word 'meteoron,' which means 'phenomenon in the sky.' It describes a streak of light with incandescence that results from atmospheric friction. It usually occurs from eighty to a hundred kilometers above earth, and there are fifty to seventy of them a day. We think that over a million have actually hit the earth's land surface."

"Has any *person* ever been hit by a meteorite?" Tomas asked.

"Only one that I know of – Ann Hodges. She died in Alabama in 1954."

"Quite a wealth of knowledge you have there. I never knew there were people who spent their lives studying meteorites." Maria picked up on the snide timbre in Tomas's voice, but hoped that her colleague had not.

"Well," John said, "the main reason we study meteorites is to determine the origin of the bodies that they came from." From the faraway look in his eyes, Maria could tell that he had not picked up on Tomas's sarcasm. It would not have mattered to John anyway; he was more than willing to speak on the subject for any reason. It was pure joy for him just to utter the names of rocks aloud.

"It's all *very* fascinating," Tomas interrupted.

"Yes," John said dreamily. "I'll do radiometric dating on the samples we'll take from this meteorite, and we'll know exactly what year it came down."

Dr. John Pippins could talk for hours about meteorites. He had a vague sense that he might have seemed strange to others, but he was a planetary geologist, and from his own point of view, he had one of the greatest jobs in the world.

They finally pulled up to their campsite. After the long trip over rough terrain, most of the weary travelers were ready for some rest. John, on the other hand, could not hold back his enthusiasm any longer. He had to go see the meteor's crash site. "I'm heading over, just for an early glimpse. Do you want to come along, Maria?"

"No, I need to get my equipment ready for tomorrow. There will be plenty of time."

"Well, how about you then, Sarah?"

"Absolutely, Daddy. Let's go." She swung her daypack over her shoulder. "Can Mae Ling come?"

"Sure she can."

Mae Ling was eager to see it as well, but she hesitated. "I'm supposed to set up camp for you," she said.

"No, you go on, Mae Ling. Tomas will help," Maria said. Tomas grimaced.

It was a half-hour walk, but once they got there, John was beside himself. "Look at it," he breathed.

"It's smaller than I thought," Sarah said. "Why isn't anyone guarding it?" She had envisioned the Chinese Army and barbed wire.

"No one really knows about it, except for a handful of scientists. It's been here for millions of years, but we are among the first people to see it. But others will come soon enough."

John turned and noticed that Mae Ling was touching the rock. "No, Mae Ling," he said sharply.

She jerked back, and scratched her palm on the jagged edge. She quickly tucked her hand behind her so that they would not see that she was bleeding.

"You must not touch it. You don't know what could be inside – or on it."

"Sorry, Dr. Pippins."

"It's okay. Remember, safety first. Tomorrow we'll have to use our gloves."

They walked around the site, as John scribbled away in a small notebook. After a while, he looked up at the sky and said, "We'd better be getting back. Dark soon."

On the way back to the camp, Mae Ling made sure that she walked behind the other two. Her blood had made a small stain on the front of her shirt, and she made sure to keep her pack over it, until she could get to her tent and change. It was just a small cut, and there was no need to let on that anything had gone wrong.

4

The next two weeks in camp went by without incident. John and Maria were ecstatic, running around like children, comparing notes, and sleeping soundly each night in anticipation of the next day's adventure.

Sarah, on the other hand, was starting to lose interest in the whole thing. Writing her report had absorbed her attention for a time, but it didn't take long before she realized she had absolutely nothing more to do. Mae Ling could have been someone to hang out with, but due to her excessively burdensome chore list, they had had almost no time together.

As for Tomas, he was even more bored than Sarah was. He was having no fun at all, and what he had thought would be a pleasant getaway for himself and his wife had turned out to be days of watching her work endlessly, and he had become lethargic, and even more irritable than he had been at the outset of their journey.

One morning, Maria explained to him that she, John and Sarah would be visiting the meteor crash site late into the evening, to gage temperature changes and take light readings. They would pack extra sandwiches, she said, but Mae Ling would take care of Tomas's dinner, if that was all right with him. He moped about for a time, but then muttered resignedly:

"I suppose that science must have priority."

The truth was that he had been watching Mae Ling with greater and greater interest. She was lithe and light, and her skin seemed to glow with youthful energy. When the wind caught and lifted her shiny black hair, he thought she cut quite a romantic figure, for such a young girl.

So, after he had passed the long day napping and thumbing through some of Sarah's teen magazines, he emerged from his tent and looked up at the dimming sky. He could hear Mae Ling, who had been busy all day straightening up the camp and preparing meals ahead of time, humming through the nylon sheathing of her tent. He approached. She had switched on her solar lantern, and now he could see her shadow against the yellow nylon.

Moving stealthily, he lifted up her tent door and took a step inside. Sensing his presence, she turned around quickly. It took her only one look at his face to know she was in trouble.

"Oh, hi," she said. "Are you ready for dinner? I was just about to start preparing it."

As he drew nearer to her, she felt the tent close in about her. She felt like running, screaming, but she didn't know how to call for help. She had never been in such a situation, had never even really had a man kiss her. There had been a few boys in her rundown neighborhood, but this...

She turned away from him at the last moment, but he grabbed her by the waist from behind, and spoke: "You're like a fresh peach, aren't you? What a little beauty you are." Before she even knew what had happened, he had undone her baggy shorts, and they slipped to the floor.

A kind of shock was setting in, but oddly, she would remember his words with brutal accuracy for many years to come. "How old are you really? Eighteen?" He reached inside her shirt.

"Fourteen," she said.

"Stop teasing me. Everyone knows the Chinese look younger than they truly are."

She looked about her, but saw nothing she might use as a weapon. All she could do was grip the back of the folding chair she had set up for reading in the evenings.

Tomas undid his pants. He had been expecting something extraordinary, something exotic, something beyond anything he had known with the young Spanish dance students he had taken as his own, but she was just the same – too tight, too dry, too…amateurish. He looked at her limp black hair, the same hair he had so often thought of in his hours of ennui during the empty days, and now he wanted to yank it out by its roots.

Instead, he grabbed her by her hair, pulled her neck back, and by yanking on her in short, violent motions, he was able to finish inside her quickly. He pushed her away from him, but then, as an afterthought, he put his hands between her legs, reached up, and wiped the stuff across her face. She gagged and sputtered. Then he spun her around, unbuttoned her white blouse, and said, "Stand there for a moment, please." He took a few steps back, and reached into his back pocket for his small Nikon digital camera. The camera flashed.

"Now change your clothes, please," he said. "I'll have my dinner by the fire, if you don't mind."

Mae Ling did as she was told. She cleaned herself up and did her best to make dinner. It had happened so quickly, in only a few seconds, really, but a great weight seemed to have descended upon her, and her soul plummeted. There was no evidence of what had taken place in the tent – only a sharp soreness between her legs and a small spot of blood on the floor of the tent. There were no tears either. If she had cried, she believed, it would have meant she felt sorry for herself, which would mean she had hope, which would mean she had something left in life, but she didn't – especially now.

She brought Tomas's plate over and handed it to him without looking at him. He said nothing. She returned to her tent and turned off the lantern.

The research party came back quietly late in the evening. They put their gear away, bid one another a good night, and crept to their respective shelters.

"How is the dinosaur doing?" Tomas asked his wife.

"Resting comfortably," Maria said.

Tomas was groggy, but he reached out for her and found her body in the darkness. He tasted the sweat of the day upon her, but he pulled her closer. She was so tired, she had simply removed all her clothes and flung them into the corner of the tent, but she knew she might as well submit; it would save her some precious sleeping time, for he would persist until he had what he wanted. Anyway, she didn't mind. She felt herself relaxing, relaxing, floating freely under him, in fact, after the intensity of her long day. It was very dark in the tent, for there was a new moon, and so she could not have seen the dark streak of dried blood that still remained on Tomas.

Sarah had started to feel uneasy about all the work Mae Ling had to do – she wasn't getting any help. Her father had told her that Mae Ling was being paid for her services, that it might even offend her sense of honor for any of them to offer to help her with the domestic duties around the campsite. However, on one of their last mornings, when Sarah had decided to remain in camp for the day, she decided she would offer to help Mae Ling prepare lunch for the group.

"No, it's all right," Mae Ling said. "I like doing it."

"But it would mean a lot to me," Sarah said. "Maybe I could learn a bit about real Chinese cooking."

"Well…"

"Come on, I'll be your assistant. It'll be fun."

"I – I guess it would be all right." She glanced over at Tomas's tent; he was still snoring.

"Great," Sarah said. "What are we making?"

"It's called…" Mae Ling looked down and seemed to lose her train of thought. This was something else that had Sarah worried: the girl had not been herself in days. She had suddenly changed from an upbeat, even bubbly young girl into a domestic zombie who moved about the camp in her own wordless world. "It's called congee. It's also known as jook. We make it all the time, in the morning, noon, and at night, but not always with chicken. I'm serving it with chicken today for lunch."

"I know my dad and Maria will appreciate it, when they get back from a hard morning rummaging through fossils. And Tomas, too, with the way he eats."

Mae Ling did not respond. They the chicken and vegetables out of the cooler and arranged them on the little folding table which Mae Ling used as a cutting board.

"I'll cut the chicken up," Sarah said.

"Here, why don't you slice up the ginger first? I'll work on the chicken."

They worked in silence together for a while. Sarah looked up at the young girl's stoic face – there was some very deep sadness there. "So, Mae Ling, in all this time, I still know hardly anything about you. Where are your parents?"

"I haven't seen my parents in a very long time. My father was in the army, and one day he wrote my mother a letter to say that he had gotten into some sort of trouble with his commanding officer. We never knew exactly what it was. Anyway, my mother decided to ride a train all the way from our home in Jining to Chang Chia Tun to try and find out what was happening. We never heard from either of them. I was ten."

"Wow," Sarah said. "I'm sorry…I didn't know any of that."

"Of course not. How could you?"

"Isn't there anything you can do? Can't you get a lawyer or something?"

Mae Ling looked up and gave her an odd smile. "All your reading about Marco Polo and you still don't know a thing about China, do you?"

Sarah looked down. Mae Ling could see that she had hurt her feelings. "Oh, I'm sorry, Sarah. I shouldn't have said that. It's just difficult for me to talk about it. My older sister tried to take care of me for a while, but it was too much for her. Soon I had to go to a barracks to work in a clothing factory. But I was lucky – I was spotted by a supervisor for a state-run travel agency, and he asked me to come and work for him. They liked my face, they said mine was the kind of face westerners expect to see when they come to China. They gave me a small room to share with some other girls, and they taught me English and…well, and here I am with you right now."

"I don't know anything about what kind of faces people expect to see when they go anywhere, but I think you're very pretty."

"You're very sweet," Mae Ling said, and she looked up to smile, but when she did, taking her eyes for just a moment off of her work, another calamity suddenly befell her: the tip of the big knife sliced a half-inch or so between her thumb and forefinger. She did not jerk it away, but stared down at the blood trickling out among the pieces of chicken and bone.

"Oh, no!" Sarah said. She grabbed a towel and quickly wrapped it around Mae Ling's hand.

Mae Ling closed her eyes. "I wish I could say I can't believe I just did that, but the way things have gone for me lately, I'm not surprised." Cuts, scrapes, bruises –

shearing off little pieces of herself – dark thoughts – uncharacteristic accidents and pessimism had come crowding into her life since the episode in the tent with Tomas.

The towel was turning a dark pink in color. Sarah lifted it to look at the cut, but it would not close. Every time Mae Ling moved her thumb, it would separate and start to bleed again. "Well," Sarah said, "at least you can move your thumb. Looks as if you didn't cut the tendon."

"Yes, I'm sure it will be all right. I'll get the first aid kit from my tent."

"I'll get it," Sarah said.

When they had stopped the bleeding with gauze and then cleaned and bandaged the cut, Mae Ling said, "I need to finish the lunch."

"You tell me what to do, and I'll finish up for you," Sarah said.

Mae Ling reluctantly consented, and sat down by the table. "You need to add ten cups of water to the pot, and put the chicken parts in the water to boil. After it boils you will need to skim the stuff off the top."

The two of them waited for the water to boil. Sarah lifted up her hand, and licked it to taste the fresh ginger that was stuck there.

Mae Ling spoke sharply, intuitively: "Did you wash your hands after we treated my cut?"

"Whoops," Sarah said. She paused with her tongue on the back of her hand. "I'll do it right now."

"Good. We may have some unusual folk recipes in our culture, but the cook's blood is not an ingredient in any of them, as far as I know."

She washed her hands thoroughly and then dropped the chicken into the pot. The girls added three tablespoons of Chinese rice wine, half-inch-thick pieces of ginger, three scallions, halved and smashed with the flat of the knife, and a half-teaspoon of salt to one cup of long grain rice. It would have to sit for about two hours.

They chatted about various things, and for a time, to Sarah, Mae Ling seemed more like her old self. After all, they were just two teenaged girls at camp, chattering away about music, movies, boys. "So who taught you to cook so well?" Sarah asked. "Your mom?"

"It was my dad actually. He kept a big garden, during the seasons he was home, and we tended it when he was away. We always had fresh vegetables."

"Nice. Funny how you learn things you'd never expect from your father. They just refuse to fit the stereotype, don't they? I remember once when I was in the car with my dad. It was a big, four-lane highway, lots of cars. All of a sudden a family of geese appeared on the road, out of nowhere, it seemed. My dad screeched on the brakes, and pulled over into the emergency lane, and he jumped out and started shooing the geese across. There must have been ten or twelve of them. He had his arms out behind them, waving his hat. I was just sitting there in the car, of course, watching the other cars come roaring up and slamming on the brakes for this grown man and a bunch of geese. It was very tense – one lane, then two, then three, and finally they were all the way across. Then he dashed back across and jumped in the car. I was horror-stricken. We drove on, and after a few minutes he turns to me very soberly and says, 'Don't ever do what I just did.'"

Mae Ling was laughing. She said, "That's exactly what my dad would have done," and to the surprise of both of them, a solitary tear appeared on her brown cheek. Sarah put her arms about her.

"There now," she said, and she patted her back. For a moment, she had a heroic and romantic idea: she would smuggle Mae Ling back to the U.S., and they would be sisters. But just as quickly, she realized the impossibility of such a notion. The sad truth was that there was very little she could do for the girl.

When the chicken was done, they pulled it out and shredded it before returning it to the pot. They added the rice, reduced the pot to a low flame, and cooked it until it looked almost like oatmeal – another hour. After they removed the congee from the flame, it continued to thicken as it stood.

Tomas came out around ten, scratched his belly, looked at them without speaking, then poured himself a bowl of cereal and went back into the tent. John and Maria returned to camp famished, exactly at noon, as Tomas re-emerged, and they all sat down to lunch. There was very little talk, only the sounds of spoons and forks and people eating with great conviction. At last John set down his spoon and leaned back.

"I think that was the best meal I've ever had," he said. "Many more like that, Mae Ling, and I'll never leave this place."

"Thanks. It was a team effort today. Sarah did most of it, in fact."

It was Maria who finally noticed the bandage wrapped between Mae Ling's thumb and index finger. "My God!" she said. "What did you do to yourself?"

"Something very stupid," Mai Ling said. "Just a slight cut." She looked up at Sarah, as if to say 'Please...'

"We cleaned it up properly," she said. "I think she'll be all right."

"Used antiseptic?" John asked.

"Of course, Dad."

Tomas was just lifting his bowl to drain the last of his jook. "I would happily have supervised the treatment," he said, "but no one alerted me that there had been an injury."

"Hmm," Maria said. "Anyway, it's time for the good news/bad news scenario. The good news is John and I finished our work this morning. The bad news, of course, is this means we'll have to break camp tomorrow and start our separate journeys back home."

"Oh," Sarah said. "Well, I suppose it had to come sometime."

"Yes," Tomas said. "Deeply disappointing."

Mae Ling stood up. "I'll start packing then," she said. Sarah looked at her sadly – she wanted to help, but this time something in Mae Ling's tone said, *No – this is how it must be.*

The group of westerners sat silently as the young Asian girl busied herself around the camp.

A few days later, when Sarah was high above the ocean with her father, heading back to Florida, she found that she could vividly recall virtually every moment of their time in China. And she kept seeing the girl's face, the unknown, unspoken sadness. She felt mysteriously joined to her in some way, even though as those last hours had worn on, Mae Ling had seemed to grow colder and even more distant. At the airport, Sarah had asked,

"Is there some way I can keep in touch with you? Email? Snail mail? Phone?"

"You can try to contact me through the agency. Though I'll no doubt be very busy. They don't like us to take personal calls."

"I see. Well, please take care of yourself."

It was too bad. If Sarah could have seen her own future before her as easily as she could now look out the plane's window, she would have seen quite a dramatic seascape, and there would have been plenty to share with some faraway friend. She would have seen herself married within three years – to Brad! Brad – who could have guessed he would show up on the scene so soon for her! She would have seen herself at twenty-two with two children, too, two handsome boys… a bit young for that, perhaps, but who can ever predict these things? They happen when they're supposed to happen. She would have seen a lovely home, and warm family gatherings over which John, her dad – asleep next to her at this instant and still so young-looking – would preside as Grandfather. And had she been able to look a little further, she would have seen herself grieving the loss of him, a funeral, people in black clothing holding one another, weeping…

But as the plane zipped along at thirty thousand feet, and for a little while longer, she was still just 18-year old Sarah, still skinny, with her brown eyes still bright and full of wonderment as she gazed down at the golden sea below her.

5

Maria sat waiting in her gynecologist's office again. She was starting to accept these weekly visits. She had always dreaded it in the past, but it had become much more bearable now that the government was paying her 850 Euros for each appointment.

She was one of a number of select women in Spain who were now able to add significantly to their incomes simply because they were women…and were menstruating regularly. To Maria, the money didn't mean that much – she and Tomas were quite comfortable anyway – but she felt she was contributing something in her own way. For other women in other countries, it was a tremendous financial windfall that was drastically changing their lives. Tomas had said it would upset the socio-economic balance, but he did not object to the extra cash Maria brought home. He was not aware that she was tucking away most of it in a small box under their bed, to be donated back to the research effort.

The World Health Organization and international disease research facilities were approaching desperation.

They were urgently trying to find the solution to what had finally been acknowledged as a global crisis – the Negra 9 Virus. They had urged various nations to "tap" certain women with normal menstrual cycles to come in and serve as models for urgent research. Some women, even some in Maria's circle, chose not to participate. But among the poorer classes, because of the money, women were showing up in droves at their cities' clinics to volunteer themselves, and the process had become more daunting and awkward than anyone had anticipated.

Maria looked over at the girl seated next to her, who smiled.

"Isn't this the greatest thing ever?" she said. "I love this. I quit my job. I don't have to do anything anymore except come to this office and let them probe me."

"Well, no, I wouldn't say it's great, considering the circumstances," Maria said.

The girl seemed not to have heard Maria's reply. "Just think, all we have to do is spread our legs for twenty minutes, and I'm done for the whole week. I mean, except when my husband…I mean…"

"I know what you mean," Maria said. "Excuse me for saying so, but you make yourself sound so…cheap."

The girl laughed. "Even prostitutes would be happy to make this much money for twenty minutes with your legs spread."

"We're not prostitutes. We're part of a very important research effort. Don't you even know why you're here?"

"I know all that," said the girl. "But my attitude is, we don't know what will happen in the future. Might as well live for now."

Maria noticed the ring on the young girl's finger; she hadn't expected her to be married. "What will you do when you and your husband decide to have a baby?"

"I know, that's a problem," the girl replied. "If I do get pregnant, the money stops flowing."

"That's not really what I meant. I mean, aren't you afraid of getting the virus? No one seems to know much about it yet."

"I'm hoping I'm immune or something. Isn't that why we're here?"

"I – I wish I knew for sure," Maria said. "From what I read, it feels like everyone around us has already got it. I don't know, maybe we are immune for some reason, or maybe we just haven't been exposed."

The girl was thoughtful for a moment. "I know that if I get it, I'm going to be really upset that I didn't have a baby," the girl said.

Maria turned to her, "You can't have the baby if you crave the money so much. One day the money will all be spent, but a child…"

"You're right, or course. A child is priceless. How many do you have?"

Maria looked down at her own hands. *Who am I to lecture this girl,* she thought. *Am I any different, any better?* She said, "Well, my husband and I want to have one very soon. This year sometime, I hope."

"Oh, I see. My name is Cruz, by the way. My husband says that eventually the government may pay us even more, if things get worse, but he'd like to have a baby, too. It's a dilemma."

"My name is Maria. It's nice to meet you. I guess we also have to ask ourselves whether it's the best thing to bring a baby into this world right now."

She felt the girl's eyes assessing her clothes, her shoes. "You probably don't need the money, do you?"

"To be honest, I don't need the money, " Maria said. "But I'd feel guilty if I refused to take part in the study. Maybe it sounds silly, but I feel like the world is counting on me."

"I guess I am kind of selfish," Cruz said. "I should feel bad for taking the money when some girls can't even have children."

A young nurse appeared in the doorway. "Maria Escobar?" she called. "The doctor will see you now."

Maria extended her hand to Cruz. "Nice meeting you," she said. "Perhaps I'll run into you again."

"You, too. And good luck to you and your husband when you decide to get pregnant. I think you should start tonight."

Maria did not reply, but walked toward the door which the nurse was holding open for her, and she entered the long, gray corridor.

6

Tomas sat in Dr. Haman's private office, where they had been making plans. He was growing very excited over his new venture. It all seemed so easy. People always wanted to please, and they were always willing to help what they perceived as a noble cause. In truth, he thought, medicine is no different from voodoo – people are drawn in by what they don't understand. And it wasn't bank robbery; it was paperwork.

His plan seemed to him flawless, beautiful. All he had needed for it to succeed was a doctor who truly understood, who would agree with his philosophy – and then he had remembered his old friend. Dr. Haman had helped Tomas through an uncomfortable situation with one of his youngest dance students a few years ago, and through a series of subtle meetings fraught with innuendo, the two had come to understand that they had much in common. Yes, Haman was just the man he needed. After all, they wouldn't really be hurting anyone else. It only took a plan and a bit of courage.

"I suggest we begin by emailing all of your patients. But you must make it seem personal. Make each woman feel she has been selected especially. Appeal to the crusader in her."

"Joan of Arc," Dr. Haman said.

"Chosen by the God of Science." Tomas studied Haman's face. It looked kindly, genuine, but he sensed a terrible ruthlessness in the man which resonated with him. In the business world, the end always comes as a separation of assets and a parting of ways. In the underground world, it is not that easy: someone always dies.

"I suppose we should get busy then," the doctor said.

"Let's consider our overhead costs. As I've said, I'm willing to cover all capital investments. How should we proceed?"

"Well, clearly I need to have these patients come into the office. Complications often arise in such situations. It's very likely that many of them will end up on the surgical table. Very unfortunate."

Tomas gave a mock sigh. "Yet it must be done. They will no doubt quickly see the good they are doing for society. You're certain that you can remove the ovaries without endangering the health of the patient?"

Haman nodded authoritatively. "Please, my friend... In this room there is only one doctor. Let me worry about those details. For all I know, we may even have situations arise wherein such a procedure may be *crucial* to the health of the patient. Your only duty is to handle the financial concerns."

"Certainly. But in your expert opinion, what sort of value do you think those...details...might bear on the free market?"

"Well," said Haman, "these are difficult times in which we live. We will learn as we go along, I suppose. Our first step is to gather a list of willing candidates for this phase of the study."

"I see. In that case, I believe an extra 500 Euros per visit would help us to attract a number of concerned citizens. How many women can you see in a day?"

"Again, my old friend, you are venturing into an area which is mine alone. It could be that we will need additional office space. That will be your concern. But remember, I am a health care professional. We must ensure the comfort of the patient. This is not assembly line work."

"Did you say 'disassembly line'?" Tomas smiled, pleased with his joke.

"That is in very poor taste," Dr. Haman said, "but given the stress we are all under, I shall ignore it. Now, we will also need refrigerated storage units, and some time. I will draft begin drafting a letter to send out to select patients. It will call upon the noblest facets of the female psyche."

"Excellent." Tomas summoned his most sincere facial expression. "In my experience with women, I have no doubt you will find an unending supply of willing participants. After all, the future of our society may be at stake."

Dr. Haman smiled and extended his hand. It was the handshake of a surgeon – self-assured but not too firm, as determined, or so it seemed, by the hand's intuitive sense of the tasks which lay ahead.

Sarah had dropped the boys off at school. She and Patty, her best friend, were just arriving in Jacksonville for a day of shopping. They glided off of I-10, took the first exit past the dark-blue river, and turned off into the San Marco district – one of those parts of town which the real estate people had labeled "exclusive." It was true that they could find things there that they would never see in Lake City, but Sarah knew her budget. Brad had made it abundantly clear.

To her disbelief, she found a parking spot almost right away and pulled up in front of Starbucks. From where they sat, they had a choice of no fewer than six places to get coffee. Why she chose Starbucks she did not know, but like so many others, she had been hypnotized by the Starbucks appeal. She had even had Starbucks coffee in Utah, where the Mormons didn't believe in coffee.

She looked at the car next to her, and then to the van on the other side. On the van there was a blue sticker with gold writing that said, "Jesus is the answer." The car on the other side had a sticker that parodied a well-known Christian symbol and had two little Darwin feet on it. *Well, there you have it*, she thought. *The great debate still rages.*

The two of them walked in. She had no idea what to order, so she just asked for the coffee of the day – that narrowed the choices down somewhat. Her friend ordered also, and each of them got a muffin. Patty went off to wash her hands, and by the time she came back, Sarah had already opened up her laptop, connected to the internet, and was scanning the current news from the *Christian Science Monitor*.

Normally, the *Christian Science Monitor* was much like any newspaper, with pictures and text, but today the front page featured a live feed. She turned up the volume a little, but she knew all too well the tragic events that were hitting the world. Across the top of the screen, above the man, was the word "Armageddon."

It was the first time she had seen that word in a news story. Wasn't that a movie title? Or perhaps a best-selling book? Now, however, a true story had been unfolding, but sometimes she found herself agreeing with Brad's most recent remarks about all of it: it's mostly hype. Like the global warming fear mongers – who knew how much of it was really true?

Patty was saying something as she walked up. Sarah hushed her. "Look at this map. It's spreading." She turned it up a little more so they could both hear:

"We have now unequivocally determined where the virus first appeared. An international team of viral specialists has determined that it originated here about ten years ago, in this barren land near Jining, China." The man pointed to the name of the city, and Sarah's eyes grew wide.

She turned to Patty. "I was there ten years ago."

"Stop kidding," Patty said. "It's not even funny."

"No, I swear, it's true. My dad was studying a find there, of a meteor that had actually hit a dinosaur. It was probably a million to one chance, but there was actually a fossil record of a dinosaur that was struck and killed by a meteor."

"Oh, I think I remember that," Patty said. "It got a lot of news coverage. Looks like it's making the news again."

The map of the world showed the infection spreading out.

"Most of this data," the reporter went on, "is a compilation of statistics on birth rates. Many of the women who have the virus may not yet realize they are infected. By analyzing the decline in birth rates, and projecting those declines across the map, researchers have determined with 99 percent certainty that it all began right here, in this remote part of the world."

"Oh, it's remote all right," Sarah said.

"I can't believe you were actually there then."

The man moved with his pointer along the map. "Just a few months later, it would appear that the first identifiable outbreak occurred here, but with only a handful of cases," he said, pointing to Spain. The map continued to darken to indicate the spread of the disease. His pointer swept across the Atlantic. "Much more serious are the cases reported here, in the southeastern U.S., particularly in Florida, and in the West, in pockets of California."

"Oh, my God..." Sarah looked at Patty. "It was my dad and me, and a young couple from Valencia, in Spain. The wife was some sort of scientist, too. We had a guide as well – a young Chinese girl from Jining."

"Freaky," Patty said.

"That can't be. That's too much of a coincidence."

The map showed the virus's spread across the United States, with projected infections in Russia and

Africa. The reporter was saying, "Much of the world has felt the impact of this pandemic. It appears, based on our studies and the reports coming from the Center for Disease Control here and the World Health Organization, that the virus is moving more rapidly with each passing week. In many heavily populated areas around the globe, sterility rates among women are approaching 60 percent. There are indeed anomalies, such as this small region in Spain, which, ironically, is where some of the first cases of Negra 9 were reported. Most women there are still able to menstruate, although – interestingly enough – the birth rate for that area as well is hovering around zero."

"Wow," Patty said.

"Something really weird is happening," Sarah said.

"So it seems," her friend agreed. She looked around at the glare from the shop windows, the general bustle going on all about them. "One of the weirdest things about it all is that people are just going on about their business. No one seems terribly concerned. Then again, I suppose we're doing the same thing they are."

"It's the American malaise. Besides, what can *we* do? If my dad were around, he could probably explain things to us. Brad still maintains it's mostly hype. He says the press is always milking these things."

"Brad could be wrong this time," Patty said.

Sarah's fingers paused above her keyboard. "Maria Escobar!" she exclaimed.

"Excuse me?"

"Dr. Maria Escobar, that was the Spanish researcher's name. I can't believe I remembered. Hold on just a minute." She typed furiously, and like magic, the first item returned by her search was a PBS site which linked to an article written by one Maria Escobar, doctor of paleontology at the University of Valencia. "Hah! Sarah shouted. "It's right here. And her email is right at the bottom of the page, so you can send her comments. I'm going to contact her. I'll do it tonight, in fact."

"You mentioned someone else, too," Patty said. "A Chinese girl."

"That's right. Her I'll never forget. She's a totally different story. Mae Ling. She was a few years younger than me, but we connected on some very deep level. Very beautiful, very smart young girl, but she had something…something wrong. She was very sad, and just seemed to get sadder. She seemed…hopeless. I felt so awful for her."

"Maybe you can track her down, too."

Sara shook her head. "I seriously doubt it. Do you know how many Mae Lings there are in China? No, I'm sure she just got lost in the shuffle somewhere. Poor kid." Now Sarah looked closely at her friend. "What about you, Patty? Have you seen your doctor recently?"

"No…but I feel fine."

"How about your menstrual cycle? Anything strange? I mean, not to be too personal…"

Patty smiled. "Listen, sister, it doesn't get anymore personal than that. But we've been friends for too long." Now she glanced down into her coffee cup and frowned. "But I am a bit late this month. Still, that's not unusual for me."

"Oh? Well, unless your Pete has had his vasectomy reversed, I'd suggest you make an appointment soon. Just to be safe."

"Believe me," Patty said. "Pete and I are done having kids. How about you?" Patty asked. "How are things on the fertility front?"

"Brad and I are definitely done, too. But I'm still pretty regular. I saw Dr. Matthews just last week, and everything checked out. All parts still in working order for now."

Sarah looked about her. Indeed, it seemed a normal day – glaring and sticky with humidity, but that was typical. Men in business suits, insurance agents taking early lunches, women in bright spring dresses. A young girl with two extravagantly groomed poodles on a double leash...

"Sarah," Patty said. "I remember reading something about government-funded research programs in other countries through selected gynecologists and clinics. I haven't heard much about it lately."

"Yeah, I saw the same story. I know they were doing that in Spain, for sure." She gestured to her laptop's screen. "I don't think it got off the ground here in the U.S. I guess that's because we've got the big research facilities in this country already, all the army experts and hospitals and all that. I know my doctor hasn't said anything about it to me."

"There's that good old American complacency again. Status quo. Just do what they tell you." Patty took her wallet out of her purse. "I'll get the coffee this time. Are you ready to do a little shopping?"

"Born ready," Sarah said.

Late in the afternoon, when the tall, downtown shadows had lengthened and the air cooled just a bit, Sarah headed up the ramp and back onto I-10. They were weary but pleased with their excursion, even though Sarah had gone over budget slightly. She just couldn't find it in her heart to go home without those shoes; Brad would make a little show, grunt, and then he would forget about it by dinnertime.

They didn't talk much on the way back, allowing the Classic Rock station to fill the time for them – "chewing gum for the ears," as her dad used to say. When she had at last dropped off her friend and turned down her own street, she saw it right away: A huge white car sitting in front of her house, an old Ford Fairlane whose shine had long ago given up the battle. Later on, she would think, *Well, I suppose that's sort of how it would work in the movies, with them waiting for you at your house.* But the man who got out and waved to her as she pulled up – he was not like in the movies: late forties with a loud plaid coat, yellow shirt, mismatched tie...only the dark glasses looked as if they were on purpose.

He walked briskly toward her and extended his hand. "Sarah? Sarah Penn?" His grin was too toothy, too white. *Has to be a bridge,* she thought.

"Yes. Do we know one another?"

"Well, not yet. But I've been looking for you for some time. My name is Howell, and I do a bit of freelance work for a government agency." He produced an ID in a folded plastic case.

She looked at it carefully. She had learned enough not to trust just any old ID card, and certainly not to trust a stranger who arrives at your house and claims to work "for the government." She scrutinized the small print. "What is 'Inter-Med'?"

He waved his hand dismissively. "Oh, it's kind of a generic name. Just means that I work for a U.S. government research team. Virology. Think of it as the FBI with a degree in medicine."

"You don't look like a doctor to me," she said.

"Looks can be deceiving, but I understand what you're saying. I can understand it, too, if you're somewhat confused – "

"I'm not confused. Surprised, you might say. Maybe slightly alarmed. But my husband should be home any second now, and he'll help us clear this up."

"We've already made contact with Brad. He and the two boys will be waiting for us."

"Waiting? Okay, now I *am* confused. Why didn't Brad call me first, then?"

Howell waved his hand again. "I'm sorry about all the cloak-and-dagger shit...er, pardon my language, please. I mean, I'll put it this way: I'm not a spy, and you're not in any trouble. I just need you to come along with me."

"Come along with you?"

"Yep. Brad and the boys are there. Just come along is all you have to do. Just for a couple of days."

"A couple of days? You must be out of your mind. Where?"

"All right, here we go again. I feel stupid saying this shit, but...I can't tell you that. 'Scuse my language."

"Well, excuse mine, but I think you'd better get off my damn lawn."   "Okay," Howell said. "Call him. Go ahead. Call Brad. You might as well, so this doesn't turn into a pissing contest."

She rooted through her purse and took out her cell phone, and dialed her husband's number. He answered before the first ring had finished. "Brad! Do you mind telling me what's going on? Where are you?"

"It's all right." Brad's voice was calm. "The boys are fine. Everything's fine. It's just very important that you do what Mr. Howell asks you to do. Trust me."

As she talked, Howell went over to his car, folded his arms, kicked the rear tire. When she had put the phone away again, he turned to her and tried to look sincere.

"Well?" he asked.

"All right, then. Let's go. But I'll only agree if I can follow you in my car. And I need to go inside and pack a few things. And use the bathroom. And I'll need to stop for gas."

"Oh, shit," he said. "I mean, er, oh, that's all right. Hurry up. We're already running late."

Cloak and dagger. But it still wasn't like the movies. There had been no men in black. No guns produced and held to her temple. No helicopters cruising low over the highway. No being held hostage in a refrigeration truck until Tom Cruise could ride up alongside on a motorcycle and rescue her.

They had driven for about forty-five minutes and arrived in the late afternoon at Shands Teaching Hospital in Gainesville. Sarah had managed to stay behind the silly man in the plaid coat, who had driven so erratically that it had almost seemed as though he *wanted* to lose her. Her fears about her government's incompetence were coming true after all, it seemed. She saw him flash his ID at the gate to the hospital's parking garage, and then followed him up to the staff parking lot – black Mercedes, silver Porsche, several Beamers…definitely a doctors' parking lot. Only Howell's old white tank seemed out of place, and hers, too, of course, as she nestled her Toyota in amongst the fancy cars.

He took her up to a waiting room on the sixth floor, and there they were: Brad, Alex, and Ben. The boys were playing on the floor with some toy cars, but they leapt up when they saw her, and ran to her. Brad put his arms around her, and suddenly she felt something give, as all her resistance and the stress of the day simply dropped away from her. She whispered into his ear, choking out the question which had weighed on her since Howell had introduced himself that afternoon:

"It's that disease, isn't it? The virus. I have it, don't I?"

Brad said nothing.

Now there was another voice behind her. It was Howell's: "Mrs. Penn?" When she turned around, a nurse had appeared beside him. She was older – silver-rimmed glasses, dyed hair. Striking blue eyes. "Mrs. Penn, this is Anita. She'll be taking care of you now. I just wanted to thank you for your cooperation today." He extended his hand, and not knowing what else to say, she muttered,

"Thank you, too."

"Good luck," he said, and then he turned and was gone, shoes squeaking down the shiny hallway.

She was alone now. It had been a full evening of lab analyses, and the nurse was at the moment taking even more of her blood. Still, it was comforting to focus on the gold cross on the woman's chest. Even though they had not talked much, Sarah had begun to feel strangely close to Anita. She was soft-spoken and serene by nature.

Sarah sighed. "Life gets complicated, doesn't it?" she said.

Anita smiled. "It certainly seems like a lot of work trying to keep it simple, I'll admit."

Sarah closed her eyes as the needle went in her arm again. "I mean, I'd heard about it, like everybody, but I guess I never realized I'd actually get it. Not that it matters. I mean, I've had my family. It's all the other girls I'm worried about."

"Get it?"

"The virus. Negra 9. That's what all this is about."

Anita looked up at her. "You think you've got the Negra 9 virus? He didn't tell you, then."

"You mean Howell? He didn't have to tell me. I knew right away."

Anita removed the needle, swirled the contents of the syringe, and placed it in the holder on the tray with the others. "It's not what you think, Sarah. He was supposed to tell you, but I guess he forgot. You don't have the Negra 9 virus."

She opened her eyes. "I don't have it?"

"Definitely not."

"Well...why am I here then?"

"We're having a look at your immune system. Your doctor passed your file along to us. Seems he detected that you might have been exposed to the disease at some point, but your resistance to it is virulent."

"Virulent?"

"The anti-toxins in your blood are extremely efficient. They knocked this thing out with the first punch. Extraordinary. Whatever you have, it's the answer. Hope you don't mind having your blood shipped off to Washington, to Maryland…Johns Hopkins, the Krieger Center – they all want to know what makes you special, Sarah."

"But I'm not special. I'm just a mother and a wife. I didn't even finish college. My dad was a very smart man, though."

Anita placed her hand on Sarah's arm. "Well, you many not think you're anything special. But some of us are investing a lot of hope in you."

"Well, if you're thinking about using me to help boost the population, you can forget it. As I keep telling everybody, I'm all done with that."

Anita laughed. "Well, that would be a pretty hefty responsibility. Mother to humankind – it's great work if you can get it. So far, only Eve has been able to qualify for that one."

"If you believe in all that."

"I think it's no more ridiculous than some of the other things people believe. But let's start small here. If we can figure out why your body is so good at resisting an illness which is having such a tragic effect on people all over the world, then we'll be on to something."

"But I've seen the news," Sarah said. "You're not going to cure those women. Their reproductive systems are gone, obliterated, according to the experts."

"Experts. When's the last time you could put any stock in an expert on anything? Besides, in the long term, there might be another strategy. We could be talking someday soon about harvesting ovaries from healthy volunteers, implanting them in other women…who knows what today's technology might offer us?"

"Harvesting. It all sounds so…what's the word…clinical? But whatever it is, it better happen soon."

"I think we're all agreed there." Anita stood up and gathered her equipment. "It's been a long day. Everyone is tired," she said. "And then there's tomorrow. Mr. Howell has arranged a hotel room for you and your family, not far from the hospital. Let's go get you checked out of here."

When Sarah had changed into her own clothes again, and Anita had pointed her back in the direction of the waiting area, she found Brad asleep in his chair. Ben was on his lap, and Alex was sprawled in another chair across the room. She approached softly and kissed her husband on the forehead. His eyes flitted open.

"Everything okay?" he asked.

"Sure," Sarah said. "I think everything is going to be just fine."

8

Maria and Cruz found themselves together once again in the waiting room. This time there was a third woman, however, around the corner, in another seating area of the office. Maria could hear her turning the pages of a magazine.

Cruz whispered: "So, have you and your husband been trying?"

"Trying?" Maria pretended not to know what her new friend was talking about.

"Trying... Didn't your mother tell you what to do to make a baby?"

"Why? Have *you* been trying?"

Cruz smiled a naughty smile. "Let's just say I've had a change of attitude. I've been adjusted."

"Hmm. Well, Tomas has been exhausted lately. He's preparing for a dance competition in the U.S. But I'm sure that after that is all over, we'll – get back on track, so to speak."

"Oh, that's too bad," Cruz said with mock sympathy. "*My* husband has more energy than either of us needs. If he keeps going like he is, we'll have triplets, I'm sure."

The two women tried to muffle their laughter, but it echoed from the hard plaster walls. The woman behind them stood up and came around the corner. She was a large woman, with great ringlets of black curls and black eyes. She stared down at them, and Maria and Cruz lowered their heads like frightened children.

"My, my," the woman said. "Aren't you two the lucky ones. Some of us here don't have a choice anymore, you know. These days, you should regard your ability to have children as a great gift."

Maria spoke up. "I'm sorry. We didn't mean to offend you. Won't you please sit with us?"

The fiery look in the woman's eyes softened, and she sat down. "I didn't mean to eavesdrop on your conversation," she said. "And I'm not saying that what you're doing here is necessarily wrong – I mean, getting paid to come here and all of that. I'd probably do the same if I could. I'm only saying that you should not make light of your ability to become a mother. You can't take that for granted any longer."

"You're right," Maria said. "And I really am hoping to have a child sometime soon."

"Me, too," offered Cruz.

"Then I envy you both." When the woman looked up at them again, the mascara had begun to run down her cheeks in watery black lines.

At that same moment, Tomas was across town in Haman's private office, watching a swimsuit competition on the TV which the doctor kept hidden in a cabinet. He had never been better entertained in his life. It didn't strike him as bizarre that these women were roller-blading in the middle of the street in the skimpiest of bikinis. *They might as well be naked*, he thought.

The camera passed through the crowd, highlighting specific parts of the female anatomy. Apparently it was in the genetic makeup of a woman that their auto-response to having a camera held up to her butt was to bend over and shake it. All of this confirmed for Tomas what he already knew: that all attractive women secretly (or not so secretly) want to show off their bodies in public. In fact, that was one of the very few things one even needed to know about women in order to control them.

Abruptly Dr. Haman came in, out of breath and a bit disheveled. "Okay, done for the morning," he said. "Let's get to work. Do you have the papers?"

"I do." Tomas smiled and reached into his briefcase. He pulled out a substantial stack of paper. He handed half of it to Haman. "I have to go out of town next week for a competition. These are the information forms for your patients, which I gleaned from the files you gave me. All we have to do is transfer the information to these other tax forms here, and that will clear us of any potential legal consequences. We can use your computer."

"Please," Dr. Haman said. "My secretary will take care of this."

"Can she be trusted?"

"It's not a matter of trust. She does what I ask her to."

It took only about an hour and a half, even though there were roughly two hundred names with corresponding personal information. Now that they had the ball rolling, Tomas could see clearly how easy this would be. They would use the same codes every week, billing all of it to the government account afforded to Dr. Haman for his part in the viral research effort. Once they had a store of cash to cover their expenses, they could begin their other more ambitious project regarding the removal of healthy ovaries. Things were not so desperate as everyone imagined, Tomas thought.

When Haman's secretary had brought the freshly typed forms in, Tomas thumbed through them. "Are you sure this is all of them?"

"That includes even those patients whose accounts were closed, going back two years."

Tomas looked up at the ceiling, numbers running through his brain. "We must figure out a way to get more patients," he said. "I have a few ideas."

Haman cleared his throat. "Don't you think this might begin to look a little suspicious?"

"I don't think so. I think everyone is caught up in the drama of the situation. As for the government – they are notorious for their carelessness anyway. Believe me, I know. I've given lessons to the wives of some of the most important men in the Spanish system."

"I would imagine so. Now, Tomas, you know me. I am a humble man, a country doctor, really. I never expected to make a great deal of money. But given your experience and research in this matter – "

"Around sixty million Euros," Tomas broke in. "If that's what you wanted to know. I think we can clear that amount by the end of the year. Of course, there is the matter of my own wife."

"Your wife?"

"Why, certainly. She's no fool, you know. She's a very good scientist in her own right. I think she's even beginning to wonder what I'm doing with myself during these days."

"You're a professional dancer," Dr. Haman said.

"Quite true. Dancing through life – it's the only way. But no one sees the work involved. The world looks at the dancer and sees only...magic."

Having hit upon just the right word, he smiled, quite pleased with himself.

Maria looked at the other two women. Finally she said to the older one: "I don't even know your name."

"Isabel." She dotted at her big face with a tissue.

"Isabel, I'm truly sorry."

The woman looked back at her. "Thank you. You don't know what I would give to be able to have a child. I would give anything. I would accept any punishment."

"Punishment?" asked Cruz. "But you haven't done anything wrong."

"Perhaps I have, and I'm being punished."

Maria said, "I would give up my career to have a child if necessary. But I don't really have to, do I? I mean, one can have both these days."

The black tears filled Isabel's eyes once again. "So it is for you," she said. "But for me... You don't understand how this is affecting my entire family. There is not a single woman in my entire family who is able to have children anymore, and no one left in my family has a male child. It's the end for us."

"It always comes down to the man," Maria said, "doesn't it?"

"What's the difference? The man only carries the name. But my family's bloodline will die out." Her great body shook as she choked out the words. Maria instinctively put her arm around the woman's shoulders. Cruz also leaned in, and rubbed her back.

"I'm sorry," Isabel said. "I'm not mad at either of you. It's no one's fault, really. It... It is. It's Armageddon, isn't it? The time has come." Her voice became a hoarse whisper: *"Holy Mary, Mother of God..."*

Cruz's small, steady voice joined hers in unison. Maria summoned all of her will, and finally it was the child inside her, the one buried there, who had attended Mass so many times with her own mother, who spoke: *"Pray for us sinners, now and at the hour of our death..."*

Tomas had gone down the hall for some coffee and a cookie, when the idea came like a shadow inside his brain. By the time he got back to Haman's office, he was walking very quickly. As soon as he had shut the door, he said excitedly. "Doctor, what do you think would happen if it were suggested in the press that someone has come up with a vaccine? Not a cure, mind you. Just something to kindle a bit of hope."

"I'd say that my clientele would increase significantly, and immediately. It might triple. But we don't have a vaccine."

"No," Tomas said, sipping carefully at his coffee. "We don't have a vaccine. Of course, there are some who say we don't really have a crisis either."

"Yes, I've heard the conspiracy theories. That this has all been exaggerated and exploited in certain quarters for political and financial gain. But let me tell you something, Tomas: I have seen the horrific results firsthand. The Negra 9 virus is quite real."

"Hmm," Tomas said. "In any case, a disturbed world might welcome the sudden notion of a vaccine."

"That's all it would be – a notion."

"Faith, Doctor, faith." Tomas looked over the steam rising from his cup and smiled.

Isabel had managed to regain her composure. Her eyes were dry now, and she had assumed an air of dignity. "Do you know who the only apostle to visit Spain was?" she asked.

"No," Maria said. "Who was it?"

"It was James."

"I wonder why James came to Spain."

"I don't know. To help people, I suppose."

"We could use him here now. Why must we go through all of this? Why is there so much suffering?"

"I don't know, and no one knows. Suffering is sometimes useful for God in some way. We may never know the reason for it. Look at the story of Job."

"I like that story," Maria said, "God doesn't seem concerned that Job is afraid. All God requires of him is faith."

Cruz said, "I don't understand why your God would do this to us. If he's really there, why do such awful things happen to us?"

Maria said, "God may allow it, but that doesn't mean He created it."

"Is it because of sin? I don't understand sin. I don't feel like a sinner."

"We don't know," Maria said. "Only God knows."

"You don't know, she doesn't know...I don't get what the big secret is."

"Suffering doesn't always come from our sin. God doesn't judge us for what we are on earth. You don't know how your story will turn out. After we die, then we are judged. In the meantime, we have a chance to do better."

The older woman spoke up: "But God is never silent. He is always speaking to us. It's our job to try and hear him."

The nurse came out and called Maria. Maria stood up and went through the doorway once again, as the other two sat and listened to the sound of her heels fading away down the corridor.

In another part of Valencia, another nurse was calling another woman. She, too, found herself walking down a colorless hallway and into a second room. There, Dr. Haman and another man were waiting.

"Hello, Jennifer. How are we feeling today?"

She looked from one face to the other, hesitant, childlike.

"Oh, it's perfectly all right," said Haman. "This is Dr. – er, Dr. Diaz, an associate of mine. He will be observing today."

Tomas smiled politely and nodded.

Dr. Haman asked the young woman, "Have you had any pain lately? Any nausea? Anything at all bothering you?"

"Well…my breasts have been extra tender this month."

"Hmm," he said. He placed his hands on her. "Let me see. What is your opinion, Dr. Diaz?"

Tomas took over the exam; he could barely conceal his excitement. He touched the girl's breasts, lifting them, then pulling them apart and letting them swing gently. He looked into her eyes.

"I'm not sure," Tomas said.

"I think we should order a mammography," said Dr. Haman.

Tomas reached out again and softly touched her nipples with both index fingers. "I concur," he said.

9

Just past noon, Mae Ling left her small, windowless room deep in the heart of Jining. As on so many days in recent weeks, she had no destination. She would return hours later, uncertain where she had been.

When she had lost her job with the tour guide company two years ago (she didn't smile enough, they said – too shy, poor communication skills), she had gone back to her chair at the clothing factory. But work had fallen off there in recent weeks, and she had grown distracted and prone to mistakes, and they had told her to go home for a while. She could not recall when she had last eaten, but she walked for blocks and blocks in Jining, on legs which somehow continued to move despite their withering thinness.

Today she found herself in a neighborhood she had never seen before. On one corner was a large modern-looking building with shutters, but when she got close, and peaked through the shutters just right, she realized it was not a building at all but a tall stone wall. She peered in. There were tanks, missiles, and helicopters – a whole armory was in there. This was not where she wanted to be. In fact, this whole town sickened her. There was nothing for her here anymore.

She felt like a bird on a ledge, all alone in the world. No one to cry out to except God, but she no longer even believed that such a being existed. No one to listen to except God, but she had not heard that voice in so long. Now she knew it had really been only her own feeble voice, her own selfish needs and desires crying out in her brain. All was barren and silent. She had nothing left in her life.

She had no money, no food. Sometimes the soldiers passed her in the streets, and they looked at her with leering eyes, and she would think that it was time to give herself to one of them, if he would only give her a few coins, perhaps a meal in exchange. *It has come to that after all*, she thought. *This is how it happens. I am worth no more than the lowest of these.*

But then, in a moment, she had resolved herself. She would not sink to that. That would be unbearable, and even though, because of that time in the tent, she was no longer clean, she would not toss away the last scrap of her humanity. She would escape in the only way she could imagine.

She had stood on the bridge before, on her long, aimless walks about the town. It was probably only a forty-foot drop to the water, but that might be enough to snap her neck and let it all end quickly. If not, she knew that she would not have the strength to swim, even if the survival instinct overtook her. She would merely let herself go down, down into the dark depths below, and soon it would be over, and there would no longer be any sense of her miserable self – no Mae Ling. And this world would go on without her, and her life would have been of no consequence to anyone, as if she had never been here at all.

It took all of her effort to reach the top of the bridge. A car came along now and again, but there was no other foot traffic. The sky was overcast, and the mist from the river was rising, and when she stood by the railing at the top, she saw that she cast no shadow. Perhaps she really wasn't here, after all – she was just a passing shape in a series of meaningless shapes. She gripped the railing, and lifted one leg over it.

It was at that moment that she heard it. It was very clear, and she recognized it instantaneously as her father's voice, speaking her name. She dragged her leg back over and turned. He was there, just beside her, and joy flooded her body like water. He was smiling, and he wore his army uniform, which was crisply pressed and stunningly clean.

He seemed almost to glow, and when she flung her arms about his neck, she felt something warm coursing round the ring which her body seemed to make around him.

"Daddy!" she cried, sobbing. "Is it really you? Are you here?"

"Of course, I'm here," he said. "What are you doing wandering about the city this way?"

"I…I don't know. I really don't know. I'm in trouble, Daddy. I have nothing left. I've been so lonely since you and Mother left. When are you coming home?"

"We cannot come back to the old house," her father said. "But we are in a very good place. I'm sorry for you, and I'm sorry that we left, but we had no choice. Your mother and I are fine, however, and we want only the best for you."

"Did the army mistreat you? Some of the neighbors said you were put into prison. Some even said that you and Mother were dead." And when she said this, the tears came again and she buried her face in his shoulder.

"My love for you can never die," he said. "Now you must listen to me, for we haven't much time." He took her face in his hands. "Are you listening?"

She nodded.

"You must go back to the old house. I have tried to get a message to you, but I could not find you. You must go to the small patch of dirt in the back, behind the old house. You remember the big rock where you and your sister used to play?"

"Yes."

"The spot is just behind that. Get the shovel out of the shed. Dig into the ground – it's only a foot or so down."

"But someone else lives there now."

Her father nodded. "You must go at night, but be very careful. Dig into the ground there, and you will find a metal box. In that box will be everything you will need. I put it there many years ago, before you were born, and no one else knows about it."

"A box? I don't understand."

"Everything will be all right, Mae Ling. Just do as I say, and go back to the old house. I must go now." He took his hands from her face, and his image began to drift slowly away from her, moving backwards, though he did not seem to be walking. He kept his eyes on her; they were moist and dark.

"Daddy, don't go," she said. "I need you... Father!"

But he was gone – swallowed by the ever-thickening mist.

"What have we here?" The airport ticketing agent peered at Mae Ling across the counter. Then he looked again at the documents before him.

"Air China. Beijing to New York City," she said. "My passport is there, too."

"Round trip?"

"Of course."

He thumbed through her papers cautiously, then gazed at her again over his glasses. "Such a big trip for a small girl."

"I'm twenty-four," she said.

"Why didn't you book a group package? " the agent asked. "Much cheaper. You know that China has a new agreement with the U.S. regarding group tours."

"I don't want to go with a group," Mae Ling said. When the man began to go through her papers a third time, she said, "Are you afraid that I'll defect? I'm not

Fujianese, you know. This is supposed to be the new China."

He shrugged his shoulders and slid her papers back to her across the counter. "Personally, I saw nothing wrong with the old China," he said. "Any bags to check?"

"This is all I have," she said, lifting her canvas duffel bag.

"One carry-on? Two weeks in New York, and you have one carry-on?"

Mae Ling nodded.

He shrugged again. "Enjoy your trip," he said.

She found the correct gate with no trouble, and sat down in one of the molded plastic chairs. She removed the magazine from her bag and opened it again to the article. She had found it – an old copy of *National Geographic* – in the Jining Library, and when she saw the story on John Pippins, she had decided that she must keep it. She had crept through the stacks, found a window, opened it, and dropped the magazine into the shrubs below. Then, when she left the building, she had retrieved it quickly.

She had begun going to the library after she had found the box with the money, right where her father had said it would be. It was a good deal of money, clipped together with a photo of her father when he was quite young. To her surprise he was not in uniform, but wore a dark suit and a tie with a lively pattern on it, but the smile was the same. She had clutched the box to her chest and hurried back to her little room. After that, the plan had taken shape slowly, but with a sort of deliberateness, even a sense of destiny the likes of which she had never felt. She had begun to eat well again and to regain her strength. She rested, and the ache in her joints had gradually gone away. She had cleaned herself up, and had begun to renew her interest in the English language through magazines and newspapers (few as they were) in the public library, where she had run across the article on John Pippins, the geologist.

It was actually just a short obituary. He had died of heart failure on July 21st, 2004. He was most noted, the piece said, for his landmark study of the fossilized remains of a dinosaur discovered in the Gobi Desert west of Beijing, China. Geological remains in the area proved conclusively that the creature had been struck and killed by a meteor – the only known case of such an event. Then there was the line at the bottom: *Pippins is preceded in death by his wife of forty years, Olivia, and survived by his*

daughter, Sarah Pippins Penn, and two grandsons, Alex, 4,
and Ben, 2, of Lake City, Florida.

Mae Ling had not thought about Sarah in a very
long time. But now the girl's face came back to her, fully
formed, the bright eyes, the short-cropped blonde hair.
They had cooked dinner together that day, the congee, that
same day that the olive-skinned man, the one from Spain,
had…had touched her. That part she had learned long ago
to put far from her mind, but now the image of Sarah began
to return to her again and again, almost hourly, it seemed.

She did not know how far Lake City, Florida, was
from New York City, but she knew she would get there.
She had the money, and she had the will. She had a plan.

10

Sarah stepped out into the glaring light on the campus of the University of Florida. She had been meeting with research professors in the Department of Microbiology and Cell Science. Of course, she was no scientist herself, but they'd had simple questions for her – what she ate, how many hours a night she routinely slept, and so on. In any case, she was entering doors which she had not even known existed when she had been an undergrad here, before she had met Brad and had chosen to end her academic pursuits. Her father had been a little disappointed when she left school, but she had always planned to go back. Then Alex came along, then Ben, and well, the years began to slip away. Still, she wondered what Dr. John Pippins, the geologist, would say about her now.

She was not alone. A herd of news reporters was moving with her across the green grass of the Plaza of the Americas. Somehow her story and the significance of her presence here had gotten out to the press, and rather than denying it, Howell and his superiors had decided to be proactive. She was getting ready to do a television interview, and the town had been stormed by reporters from all over the country, and even some from international news agencies. There was also a group of federal Secret Service agents attached to her, which made her feel strange.

She had said to Howell: "Do I really need bodyguards? I'm not the president of the United States, you know."

"You're right," Howell had said, offering his toothy grin. "You're way more valuable than he is."

Now, as they moved across the lawn toward the steps of the Journalism building, Howell was with her again. He took her elbow and leaned close to her ear. "There's something else on the agenda," he said. "We are running an autopsy right now on a woman who is very similar to you, genetically," Howell said.

"How do you know that? Did she look like me?"

"Not necessarily. Sounds morbid, but we've asked local authorities in certain regions to start screening dead people. Asked them to look for certain characteristics. This particular woman died suddenly, hit her head in a fall down some stairs. But we've determined she's a very close match with you, biologically."

"That's comforting to her, I'm sure. Did she have kids?"

"No, and that's key. Allows for some important comparisons. Anyway, we'll have to take another DNA sample from you later today."

"Sounds like fun," Sarah said. "I wonder if she was a distant cousin or something. Where was she from?"

"Atlanta. Got any family up there?"

"None that I know of." *Fell and hit her head*, she thought. *That's how fast it can happen.* "Tell me the truth, Mr. Howell. Is any of this really leading anywhere? I mean, do they think there's going to be a cure anytime soon, or at least a vaccine?"

"Let's just say we're making some significant progress. Here we are."

Before her was a podium with a great bouquet of microphones around it, and a row of TV cameras and stacks of lights lined the sidewalk. God, she thought, *I wish Brad were here.* He had gone back to Lake City with the boys, to try and have them resume a somewhat "normal" life. She approached the podium. She had watched her father give many interviews, but had never imagined anyone might be interested in anything *she* had to say.

"Any last-minute coaching?" she said to Howell.

"Just be yourself." There was a slight whistle of feedback, the lights came up, and Howell leaned toward the microphones. "We only have a few minutes. Does anyone have a question for Mrs. Penn?"

There was a scrum among the reporters, but finally one of them got his question out: "Mrs. Penn, what is your role in the Negra 9 research program."

She cleared her throat. "Well, as far as I know, they're interested in me because I seem to be immune to it."

"What is it about you that makes you resistant when so many others are not?" asked a well-manicured woman in a crisp white suit.

"I don't know," Sarah said. "That's what the doctors are trying to find out."

"And how many children do you yourself have, Sarah?" asked a short man with very large glasses.

"I have two. Alex and Ben. They're 8 and 6." She waved at the cameras. "Hi, boys!"

There was a ripple of laughter. "Do you plan to have anymore?" someone else asked.

She looked at Howell. "That's sort of a personal question, isn't it?"

A tall, immaculately dressed man with a CNN badge asked, "I've heard a rumor that you're thinking about listing your ovaries on eBay for four million dollars each. Is that true?"

Sarah was horrified. "What?! Where'd you hear that?"

"It's been reported."

"That's the most asinine thing I've ever heard," she said. "I don't even think that's legal. Besides, it's not my objective to get rich from this."

"Then what is your objective in being here today?" asked the woman in white.

"Objective? I didn't exactly volunteer for this." She nodded toward Howell. "They brought me here."

"Who are *they*?" asked another man.

"The government. The people who are doing all the research and trying to find an answer to this terrible thing. The people who are trying to help us."

Someone in the crowd laughed. "Do you worry about being kidnapped, or that something might happen to you?" someone asked.

"No, I don't worry about that. I can't imagine there is a living soul that bad. We're talking about the future of our society. There's no question that this is real. Birth rates have declined across the country...around the world for that matter."

"Do you see yourself as a modern-day Eve?" asked the tall CNN reporter.

"Eve?"

"Sure, you know – Adam and Eve. First woman, first mother, all that."

"I hadn't thought of it that way."

"Are there any other women like you, Mrs. Penn?" asked the woman. "Any there others who've been proven to have immune systems like yours?"

At this point Howell stepped up to the mic again. "She can't comment on that. Privacy laws prevent us sharing files on any other patients at this time, and Mrs. Penn wouldn't know them anyway."

"So there are others?"

"I would say we shouldn't discount any possibilities. Thank you, ladies and gentlemen. Mrs. Penn has another appointment to keep."

He led her away by the arm, as the Secret Service agents huddled about them and moved in formation. She whispered: "*Are* there others?"

"I can tell you that we have great interest in at least one other woman."

"Where does she live?"

"Well, if you don't know anyone in Georgia, you certainly won't know anyone in Spain."

"Spain? Where in Spain?"

"Valencia," he said.

Her secret settled in her heart, they passed beneath the trees along the quay: light, shadow, light, shadow. "I hear they're famous for their oranges," she said.

11

The autopsy had been completed, and Dr. Curtis and Dr. Eastman, two of the university's most prominent microbiologists, were running the lab analysis. As they examined the results, they entered into that comfortable silence which exists between professionals who know one another's work well, until Dr. Curtis said:

"It's like a locust."

"Yes," Eastman said. "Each fiber seems to move independently, and then suddenly something triggers it, and they all start forming together. It's bizarre."

Curtis peered through the microscope once more, hoping to see something that would make sense to him, but after a few moments he looked up at his colleague and removed his gloves. "John," he said, "I don't know about you, but I'm ready for a coffee break."

"Absolutely," said Eastman.

The faculty lounge just down the hallway was a welcoming haven of disheveled newspapers and overstuffed recliners, in deliberate contrast to the exacting and sterile atmosphere of the lab. Curtis filled his partner's heavy ceramic cup, and then poured his own into the "Number One Dad" mug his four-year old daughter had given him. He shook his head.

"I guess we're gonna need a miracle on this one." He smiled wryly, knowing his friend would take the bait, as always.

"We *are* the miracle, Tim," Eastman said.

Their discussions of religion and science dated back to their days sharing a dorm room as undergraduates, when the late-night study sessions always wound up in philosophical diatribes. Each man had deepened in his convictions: Tim Curtis was a devout Methodist, while John Eastman did not hesitate to pronounce his atheist views at every opportunity and in any company.

"What do you mean, John? I don't follow you."

"Oh, I'll grant you, miracles still have entertainment value," Eastman said, "but even I know that Jesus thought miracles were too showy. He relied on parables, mostly, but I guess he performed a miracle from time to time when he thought it was absolutely necessary."

"I bet Lazarus was glad he did," Dr. Curtis said.

"Maybe. Anyway, it's the scientists, our homies…we're the ones pulling off the closest things to miracles these days. Don't they call God the great physician?"

"Well, yeah, but you don't believe in any of that. Strange the way you talk so knowledgeably about it, yet you don't buy it."

"Aw, hell, Tim, I know a lot about football, too, but that doesn't mean I'm a fanatic."

"Nice," Curtis said. "Football as religion. Always been part of the code of the South."

"I'll say one thing," Eastman said, "If we pull off your so-called miracle on this one, we're definitely *not* keeping it a secret. I don't care what the feds say, I'm telling everybody."

"Still thinking about that Nobel Prize, huh?" Curtis joked.

"You get money with that, you know."

"Oh-ho, the money. That's what this is all about? Didn't you see the TV interview with the Penn woman this morning? It's all about saving civilization." He gestured to the television suspended in the corner of the lounge. The story was still being replayed on all the cable news networks.

"Oh, yeah, the egg woman. I saw that. She's not bad-looking, but you might say we're putting all our eggs in one…basket? A tisket, a tasket, I *like* her little basket."

Curtis shook his head again. "You're a sick sonofabitch, you know."

"Could be," said Eastman, rinsing out his cup, "but I'm going back to work."

"I'll be with you in a couple of minutes. Gotta call Karen, let her know we're working late again this afternoon."

As his colleague disappeared through the door, Dr. Curtis took out his cell phone. As she always did, his wife answered with her familiar "Hi, babe."

"Hey. Just wanted to make sure you can pick up Jen today… Yeah, I've gotta stay late… Well, I'm not sure, I…have to help some students with a project." It pained him not to be able to tell her the truth about what he was working on, but that character from the state department had told them in no uncertain terms not to mention it to *anyone*.

He squinted up at the TV. It was a different news story now. The camera panned across thousands of people on their knees on the grassy mall in Washington, D.C., with the various monuments and buildings looming in the background. "What in the world…" Curtis muttered.

"How's that, hon'?" Karen said.

"Oh, just something on the news in the lounge here. Bunch of people in Washington. They seem to be praying."

"Oh, yeah," she said. "I saw the same thing. They're doing it in New York, too, in Central Park. I think somebody declared a day of prayer, for a cure for that Negra 9 virus thing."

"Oh, right," Curtis said. "I hope it does some good. Gotta go. See you tonight."

He went to the sink, splashed his face with water, then dried it with a paper towel. He rubbed his eyes. "God, I'm tired," he said.

He made his way back down the hall to the lab. He opened the door to find Tim Eastman sitting on his stool, staring blankly at the far wall. His face was ashen.

"John, you okay?"

Dr. Eastman looked over at him. "Yeah," he said. "You won't believe me, but I think I just figured something out. I was just sitting here, and it hit me, all of a sudden."

He pointed at the microscope. "Come look at this thing again, and I'll explain."

Curtis approached, leaned over, put his eye to the microscope, and gazed down the barrel to the past, the future, and the terrible moment at hand.

12

Maria Escobar sat at her computer in her office at home, looking through some digital pictures from the various vacations she and her husband had taken together. She was taking stock of the great life they had had, a life they had led on their own terms. It had been a great deal of fun; she'd had exciting things happen in her life. She had felt she had learned a great deal, too, and had accomplished many things in her professional life. But she could almost feel it was slipping away from her. It was as if she were trying to grasp something, but whatever it was flowed right through her clasping fingers. She had decided it was time to have a talk with Tomas about children.

It was strange how she had come to this conclusion; it was after she saw a motorcycle advertisement in a magazine that said, "Make yourself a star." She didn't know exactly what it meant, but a few moments after she had seen the ad, she thought to herself, *I'm going to make a star*, meaning a baby. She wanted a bright light in her life, something wonderful, something only she could help to create.

As she sat there, ruminating over all of this, a pop-up on her screen told her she had just received a new mail message. She switched over to email, and opened it up. The message was from someone named Sarah Penn. *Never heard of her...must be more spam*, she thought, but just as she was about to press the delete key, she saw the opening phrase of the email:

"You probably don't remember me. I'm the former Sarah Pippins..."

Now there was a blast from the past. Sarah Pippins.

"...and about ten years ago, you and I spent a few weeks together in the Gobi Desert. My dad, John, was there, and your husband Tomas, and a young Chinese girl named Mae Ling..."

The message was a bit chatty, but there was also an undercurrent of urgency about it. She asked that Maria get back in touch with her as soon as possible, as there was an important matter she wished to discuss, and so as soon as she had read through her other emails, Maria wrote a quick note back, asking Sarah if by chance she had a web cam so that they might renew their acquaintance through a video conference. Another check of her email ten minutes later showed that Sarah was still on line: *"Sure,"* she wrote. *"My husband, Brad, just has to have all the latest techno-gizmos. I used to talk to my father all the time by web cam. I'll log into messaging right now. What's your screen name?"*

Easy as walking across the street, Maria thought.

Within a few moments, a bright, pretty face appeared on her screen. *Yep*, thought Maria, delighted, *that's her, all right.*

"Hello, Sarah. You look very well. You're all grown up, I see."

"Hi there, Maria!" Sarah effused. "How's this for long-distance service? You look very well yourself. I was just a kid when we last saw one another."

"That's right. I read about your father's passing a few years ago in one of my journals. I'm so sorry for your loss. He was a wonderful man."

"Thanks. It was a tough time for us. I've got a great support system here, terrific husband, two boys. They're everything I ever wanted."

"I'm very happy for you, Sarah."

"How's your work going?"

"Work is good," Maria said. The truth was she didn't want to talk about work at all. She felt far removed from all of that at the moment.

"Well," Sarah said, "I guess I should get right to the point. I mean, it's wonderful to be in touch with you again, but I do have another reason for contacting you."

"Oh?"

"Yes. I suppose you've heard of the Negra 9 Virus."

Maria smiled. "Heard of it? You might say that. Let's just say my gynecologist has made a pin cushion out of me. I've been stuck and prodded and x-rayed in more places than I knew I had."

"Oh, really? I don't mean to get too personal right off the bat, but do you mind my asking why? I've sort of been experiencing the same thing here."

"I don't mind at all," Maria said. "It seems they can't figure out why I'm so healthy. Lots of women here have been affected by the virus."

"Lots of them?" Sarah said, "Or all of them?"

"Not all. The news reports say there are many women in this part of Spain who can still get pregnant."

"Yes," Sarah said, "I hear the same reports around here. The thing is, I don't know any of them. Tons of people I do know – at least the ones who have been tested – they're all now being treated for Negra 9. It's been devastating to us."

"Well," Maria said, "I don't know that many people at all anymore outside of the university. Unless you count the women who come into the clinic."

"Are any of them still having normal menstrual cycles?"

"Well...no." Maria frowned. "But you know how some girls are. What's a 'normal' cycle anyway?"

"Okay," Sarah said. "But I think you and I have to face the fact that we are part of a small minority of women which is growing even smaller, as this thing spreads. As far as the so-called experts here can tell, for some reason, I'm immune to Negra 9."

"Hm. My doctor has told me the same thing."

"Look, Maria, you're the scientist here, but do you...?"

"Do I think it has anything to do with our trip to the desert? Is that what you wanted to ask me?"

"Yes. It's the only thing I can think of. That was the last big trip I ever took, before Brad and I got married and settled down. We went to Mexico for our honeymoon, but other than that, I've been right here for the longest time. I – I just can't think of any other explanation. And if you're going through the same thing I am…"

"What about the other girl? What was her name again?"

"Mae Ling," Sarah said. "I've tried to reach her. I contacted the tour company that booked her as our guide. I even contacted the U.S. embassy in Beijing, but no one has any clue who she is. It's as if she dropped off the face of the earth."

"I hate to be the one to say this," Maria said. "but there is a chance she could be deceased. Mortality rates for young people are still high in some parts of China. Some of the hospitals are inadequate."

"It would be hard for me to believe that," Sarah said. "She was so intelligent, and obviously very talented. Her English was better than mine, and she pretty much ran the camp, even though she was only what, fourteen at the time? Still, I guess there was something tragic about her.

Some secret she was keeping that seemed to be crushing her."

"You knew her better than I did," Maria said. "I still have a few contacts in China through my research. I'll see what I can do to try and locate her. God knows how many girls named Mae Ling there must be in that country."

"One other thing, Maria. Has anything unusual happened to you lately? Government officials contacting you, anything like that?"

"No, I don't think so."

"How about at work?"

"No, I'm not teaching any classes this semester. I haven't really been near the university for several weeks."

"That's good to know. But now it occurs to me that as long as you're on sabbatical, you might as well come to the States for a visit. Our climate here in Florida is probably about what you're used to. And I'd really like to talk about some of this in person with you."

"Thanks for the invitation. Very gracious of you, but it's just not possible for me right now. I think you need to calm down and not worry so much. Be patient."

Sarah spoke softly: "There are a few things going on here that I can't talk about right now. I'd really like to see you."

"I appreciate your situation," Maria said, "but it's just not a good time for me to travel. My husband and I have a few issues to sort through. It so happens he's retiring from professional dancing and teaching next week, and we're throwing a big party."

"I see," Sarah said. "Well, perhaps in a few months, once things settle down for you there."

"Sure. In the meantime, each of us knows where the other one is. I'm so glad we were able to renew our friendship. That trip to China was quite an experience."

"It certainly was. I think about it all the time. It was the last time I really got to spend quality time with my dad. I miss him more than I ever thought I would."

"I'm sure he's watching over you," Maria said. "I'm sure he's very proud of you and your sons. Give them a big kiss for me."

"I'll do that," Sarah said. "Stay in touch, Maria."

And with a click, the face was gone. Sarah Pippin faded back into her own life. For an instant, Maria felt bereft, forlorn. She looked around her office, with its half-open books and notepads lying about, the photos of Tomas. "Now where has that thing gone?' At last she spotted it – the little red-covered Bible. Her progress through it this time was slow, but each day the time she spent with it in hand seemed more precious to her. She opened it to the place she had marked this morning:

Exodus – 34:6. "And He passed in front of Moses. The Lord, the compassionate and gracious God, slow to anger, abounding in love and faithfulness, maintaining love to thousands, and forgiving wickedness, rebellion and sin. Yet he does not leave the guilty unpunished; He punishes the children and their children for the sins of the fathers to the third and fourth generation. "

But that was the Old Testament God. Things were different, under the new covenant. Her God would not punish the children of the latter generations.

She replaced the book, turned back to her computer screen, and performed a Google search:

Popular baby names

For Sarah's part, she was frustrated by her conversation with Maria Escobar. *Stubborn lady*, she thought. Once again, she was amazed by the resistance she seemed to encounter at every turn. What was it with people? Could they not see what was happening all around them?

She went back out to the den, where the TV was now on almost constantly. Since she had returned home from Gainesville, she found herself obsessed by the news channels. Day and night, she heard the sordid tales of hospital kidnappings, live car chases, senseless violence. And the Negra 9 Virus; there was something regarding that nearly every hour. Nearly every day, she saw a replay of her own interview on the steps of the University of Florida journalism building. It was very strange, as if the woman on television and the person now sitting on the couch had become two different people. It gave her a sickening sense that the reality might actually be the image on the screen: that person seemed alive, vivid, whereas she herself was like a shadow, and empty.

The word "ALERT" appeared at the bottom of the screen as the camera cut to the now familiar image of the world map with the ever-expanding black tentacle-like lines reaching into all crevices and countries. The man in the gray suit was talking again:

The Center for Disease Control in Washington has issued a guarded statement announcing a possible breakthrough in the search for a cure or vaccine for the Negra 9 Virus, the pandemic which has caused fear and even panic in virtually all parts of the globe. Speculation about the true prevalence of the disease and the manner by which it is transmitted has generated both bitter divisiveness and a sense of unity in places as widespread as California and India. The impact on the international stock and exchange markets has been significant as well, and corruption in state-funded laboratories has resulted in personnel overhauls in at least two leading research facilities, but today's news was welcomed on all fronts.

Officials say that two research scientists within the University of Florida's Microbiology Department were responsible for the new information, although the CDC declined to name the scientists. The report suggests that a comparison between samples taken from a deceased Negra 9 victim and bacteria found in dinosaur DNA, of all things, taken from a sandstone fossil in Montana in 2005, showed striking similarities. Government agents have undertaken the daunting task of contacting anyone who might have been exposed to the 70-million year old soft tissue of a

Tyrannosaurus Rex found by researcher Mary Higby Schweitzer three years ago. We'll have further details for you as they emerge...

Well. Sarah sat back on the couch and blinked. So, the dinosaur connection was not insane, after all. But how did they come up with Montana? She flipped through the other news stations; all were reporting the same story, but none made mention of the meteor crash site near Jining, China. Perhaps Maria was right, and all Sarah really needed was a good long rest. Still, that wouldn't happen today.

She crept back to the bedroom, where Brad was still sleeping soundly, and looked at the glowing red digits: 4:15 a.m. She went to the boys' rooms, first Ben's and then Alex's. Even for such a rowdy pair, sleep brought that angelic countenance. Today was a school day. The brief luster of their celebrity status, their boasting that their mother was now a TV star, the famous egg woman, had worn off. They were back to being Ben and Alex.

She went to the kitchen, turned on the coffeemaker, and tried not to think about dinosaurs.

13

A huge night had arrived in the lives of the Escobars. They were celebrating Tomas's final performance, in an ornate but rather small theater in their own town of Valencia. He had danced well all evening, and as soon as the competition was over, he would announce his retirement, the end of his career. He saw himself standing at the edge of some glorious second life, some sort of reincarnation, although he was not yet quite certain of all that this would entail. Maria had become convinced he was serious about starting a new career as a guitarist, although she knew the reality of it was distant from his abilities. On the other hand, Maria - with their financial life more stable than it had ever been, and her anticipation of Tomas's renewed attention to their home life - had begun to believe even more firmly that this was the right time for them to have children. Still, they had not discussed the matter.

She watched him move around the floor with his partner; it was very different from his rehearsals. When she watched him rehearse, she took it all too personally, though she did not wish to; simply put, it was hard to watch him holding another woman in his arms. But here, in performance, and in front of all these people, it was beautiful. She was proud of him, and she was still amazed at what he could do with his feet, his legs, his shoulders, and his back.

Her love had always remained strong for him, but when he danced, she regressed to a state of infatuation. By the dim light in the hall, he seemed a figure out of some gothic romance. She looked through the crowd, watching all the people watch her husband. She enjoyed seeing their smiling faces, but even more, she liked it when they applauded. Some movie stars command a huge following, she realized, but she perceived something much more intimate about pleasing a few hundred people than pleasing ten or twelve thousand people; also, there is a more heightened emotional involvement with the dance.

She also knew that the next few months would be an odd period of adjustment for him. He had quite an ego, that was certain. She wasn't entirely sure how he would handle it. The crowd loved him, and he loved them back - especially the women.

His final moment came. Tomas and his partner stopped and looked out at the audience. The people immediately stood up and cheered, for they knew that this was the culmination of an artist's career. For Maria, it felt like the end of a long journey. What would they do? How would their lives be different?

There was a café adjacent to the theater, and afterward, as they sat at a small table with a bottle of wine, a reviewer from a major European arts magazine, a petite, attractive brunette with great, glistening eyes talked with Tomas in a giddy tone: "How did it feel tonight, Tomas?"

"It felt good, very good, very good. I could have danced all night."

It took her a moment to comprehend the reference, but when she did a gale of laughter swept over her. Then she asked, "Do you think you might come out of retirement someday? You seem to me as agile as ever."

"Yes, catlike, wouldn't you say? Quite seriously, though, I want to stop before I am too old, before my body refuses to cooperate. When I first started my career, so many years ago, I decided that I never wanted to be one of those performers who kept dancing past his prime, one who is constantly looking over his shoulder to see who is coming along to outdo him. I ask that everyone remember me as a great and wonderful young dancer, not as an old man who doesn't know when to quit."

"What will you do now, Tomas?" the reviewer asked.

"That's an interesting question. I have taken up a study of classical guitar. Perhaps something will come of that one day."

"I didn't know you played guitar."

"I haven't been able to practice as much as I'd like to, but that should change as of tomorrow. I'll be practicing night and day, and soon you will see me in performance again. Five years from now, I shouldn't be surprised if I am back on this stage, playing the guitar for all of these people."

"But mustn't one begin learning guitar at a very young age?" the writer asked. "Just as you did with dance?"

"Well, I have a thorough grasp of the musical theory behind it. I have the theory, the knowledge, the will... I just need to get my fingers in shape. Before it was my thighs, my calves, my buttocks, but now it's the fingers. Merely a matter of adaptation."

"What about you, Maria?" For the first time, the brown-haired woman turned to her. "What are your thoughts about your husband's retirement?"

"Oh, I think it will undoubtedly be nice for us to be able to enjoy some family time together."

"Ah, you mention family." The woman smiled at Tomas. "With your...extra time, do you think maybe you'll have children now?"

Maria felt the heat rising in her face. "Given the situation in the world today, I don't really think that question is appropriate," she said.

"I can answer that," Tomas said. "No, we shall not have any children. Maria is too dedicated to her work at present, and as I said, I would like to pursue my other interests. Children just wouldn't fit into our lives."

Maria looked at him sharply, then realized that he was not to blame. They had not had time to talk things over, and he was merely repeating the sort of thing they had both been saying for years.

"Well," said the writer uncomfortably, "I certainly wish you well with whatever you decide."

A little later in the evening, when everyone around them had had lots of champagne and wine, and things were quite loud, she whispered in his ear: "Perhaps it *is* time we talked about a baby?"

He recoiled from her. "My God," he said. "You're not…"

"No, I'm not pregnant. But I think I'm ready to be."

Tomas's voice grew louder. "Why are you talking about children tonight, of all nights? You've never brought this up before. We have always agreed that we don't want children."

"I know, I know, but I've been thinking. That I am able to have a baby right now is a gift to us. Not everyone has such a gift these days."

"Oh, I see," he said. "It's the news – those ridiculous stories. Most of it has been exaggerated by the American media, and their so-called journalists. Well, we cannot live our lives based upon what you see on television."

"It's not just that." Maria could hear her own voice breaking, and she fought to control her emotions. "I – I really do want a child in my life."

"Have you forgotten about the money? If it's true that things are getting worse, we'll earn a fortune, as long as your doctor is correct in his speculations about your immunity to this virus…if it does exist."

"I *am* immune," Maria said. "I just have a feeling about all of this, Tomas. It's as if, for the first time, I feel I actually know what I'm supposed to do. And it doesn't involve earning a fortune."

"That's crazy talk," he said. "You with a ph.d, and you say you don't know what you are supposed to do. You are supposed to do your work. Again, why do you bring this up tonight, of all nights?"

The argument escalated.

Finally Tomas said, "I'll see you at home. The evening has been ruined." He stood up, chair toppling backwards, and stormed off. She knew she should go after him and calm him down. She wasn't only worried about tonight; she was worried about everything, the timing of it all. He was probably already feeling fragile, she thought, walking away from the only life he had known for so many years. She was thoughtless to have brought it up. She decided at that instant to dismiss the idea of a child from her mind forever, and she really hoped that this would be the end of it, but she was afraid that it wouldn't. There was a half-bottle of wine remaining on their table, and she poured herself a glass.

The she thought, *No, I need to go home. I must follow Tomas. He is all I have.* And lifting her skirt just above her knees so that she would not trip, she hurried after him. But it was too late – he had already disappeared into the night.

14

So, it had not gone so well. As Maria pulled the
blankets up to her chin, she was thankful that she had at
least had enough sense not to say anything else. She had
merely come home, found Tomas already in bed, and she
had put on her nightgown and crawled in beside him. The
two of them lay there in silence for a while, until Tomas
got up, put on his slippers, and went out onto the balcony.

She would never be quite clear about exactly what
happened next. Five minutes or so had passed, and then
she heard noise outside the French doors, a scuffle. Male
voices. She froze. There was an intruder on the balcony,
and Tomas was in trouble.

She heard him say, "What are you doing here?" and
then there was a muffled report, a sound like someone
hitting a rug with a stick. Then, all was quiet.

She sat up and cried, "Tomas! Are you all right?"

He did not answer. She peeked out through the
sheer curtain, and saw his shirtless figure prone on the tile
floor.

She would never even remember picking up the phone and calling emergency services. She would, however, remember the sound of the sirens, something she had heard in the nighttime before, but it had always been for someone else, some poor soul she would probably never meet. This time, they pulled up to the Escobar house, with flashing red lights and a wailing that was almost unbearable. She opened the door for the officers and paramedics and pointed to the balcony, and then she sat down on the bed and tried to breathe.

Maria waited at the police station in a sparse little room, in a hard plastic chair, with yesterday's newspaper on a formica coffee table. She was almost able to smile when she realized how similar it was to the waiting area at her gynecologist's office, but mainly she just stared at the floor. Once, the door opened, and a man in a wrinkled suit looked in at her, squinting.

"Just checking," he said, and as the door was closing, she saw behind him two people seated in identical chairs beside an identical formica table in the next room. One was her neighbor, Señor Juarez, who looked up at her and waved. The other was that woman, the reviewer for the arts magazine who had spoken with them at the café, after Tomas's show. She was looking at a small black planner.

At last, around two in the morning, she was ushered into a detective's office. It was the man in the suit, behind a large desk, with a nameplate that read 'Captain Mendes.' In another chair was a man in a red polo shirt and blue jeans, who looked as if he hadn't slept or shaved in some time.

"I need to see my husband immediately," she said.

"What hospital is he in, Señora?" asked the man in the suit.

"That's what I need to know," Maria said. "The paramedics wouldn't even talk to me, and I don't have a car. I have no idea why your officers brought me here."

The detective's tone seemed condescending. "It's obvious, isn't it? You witnessed a crime."

"I didn't see anything," she said. "I just want to know where my husband is."

He turned to the bleary-eyed man. "Go and find out which hospital Senor Escobar is in, please." The other man rose slowly and ambled from the room.

"Why didn't you ride in the ambulance?" Mendes asked.

"They wouldn't let me."

"Seems a bit unusual."

"I have an even better question," Maria said. "Why am I here, when I should be with him?"

Detective Mendes leaned back in his chair. "Where were you, precisely, when your husband was shot?"

The word made her heart race. "Shot? I wasn't sure he had been shot. I did hear a – a sound, but I was inside. Tomas was out on the balcony, just off of our bedroom."

"I see. Why was he on the balcony?"

"He...he often goes out there at night. And we'd had...a slight tiff."

"A tiff?"

"Yes, we had argued. Nothing too serious."

"If you don't mind my asking – can you just give me a general sense of this...tiff? What was it all about?"

She sighed and looked away. "I don't even recall now, to tell you the truth. Something silly, no doubt." She had never been a very good liar, and she knew it.

"I see," said Mendes.

"Were you and your husband drinking tonight, Mrs. Escobar?"

"*Doctor* Escobar," she said.

"Sorry. Were you and your husband drinking?"

"Very little. A few glasses of wine. It was a retirement party."

"Retirement? So young."

"Tomas is a professional dancer," she said. "It's not unusual for someone in that line of work."

"Quite right. Do you and your husband have such disagreements often?"

Maria leaned forward. "Listen," she said. "It's clear what you're getting at, but I'm telling you, I was in the bedroom, and Tomas was on the balcony. It should be perfectly obvious to anyone who knows us that I love my husband very much – "

The unkempt man returned, went behind Mendes's desk and whispered into his ear.

"You're sure?" Mendes asked. "You checked Malva-Rosa? Sagunto? The university hospital?"

"All of them," the other man said.

Mendes frowned. "That's odd."

"What's the matter?" Maria asked.

Mendes forced a smile at her. "Oh, just a slight bit of confusion. We're not quite sure at the present moment which hospital your husband was taken to."

She closed her eyes. "This is not happening," she said. "This can't be happening to us."

"Well," Mendes said. "I'm sure there is just some mistake. Sometimes it takes a little while for the paperwork to be pushed through, in an emergency situation. In any case, I'm sure that he is in good hands. Medical care in Valencia is quite good."

"This is unbelievable." Maria put her face in her hands. She could no longer help herself – she began to cry.

"There, there," the detective said. "I think it would be best if you go home now. I'll have Officer Sanchez here take you. As soon as we know something, we'll send someone for you."

"But – I don't want to go home. I want to know where Tomas is."

"Of course. But it would be best for all concerned for you to return home and wait to hear from us." Sanchez tried to manage a sympathetic smile. "There's nothing you can do here. You'll be much more comfortable in your own house."

She could not resist any further; all of her strength was now drained. She allowed herself to be led by the arm outside and into a police car. As she sat there in front seat silently crying, she kept her face hidden. But it didn't matter: the tired-looking, unshaven man never even glanced over at her.

The house was quiet and dark, the colorful edifice with its flowers and tiles now merely a series of mottled gray shades. Robotically, she went back to the bedroom, undressed, and got into the cold sheets. She thought to herself: *Shouldn't they have sent a guard with me? What if whoever it was that attacked Tomas returns?* There were no weapons in the house – maybe a couple of sharp knives in the kitchen.

She lay there for what seemed a very long time, watching the numbers click over on the digital alarm clock. Finally, at 5:15, she got up, took a warm shower, put on her bathrobe, and went into the living room. There was Tomas's guitar, leaned in the corner – she went over and brushed the strings with her fingertips. Where was that little red Bible of hers? This would certainly be the time to seek solace in it. She looked under the magazines stacked on the table, and then she went into her office and looked in all the desk drawers and on the bookshelves. Not there. She sat down in her swivel chair and gazed at the picture on the desk of herself and Tomas. They were at the seaside, smiling, fit, happy; he had his arm flung across her shoulders, and her hand was on his bare chest.

They had spent a great deal of time by the water in those early days. In fact, they had met at a lake with a sloping, grassy beach. She had been alone, lying on her stomach on a towel, when a man flipped a peseta onto the small of her back. She reached back for it, examined it, and then looked up at the man.

Tomas had smiled at her and said, "Oh, I'm so sorry!" He was standing next to her, a few feet away, with a male companion. "My friend here and I were flipping this coin to see who was going to ask your name. We're both extremely shy, so we thought we'd flip for it. Was it heads or tails?"

"I don't know," she said. "What did you call?"

"Tails," he said, grinning. The sunlight gleamed in his black hair, and his teeth were very white.

"As a matter of fact, I think it was tails," she said.

"Seňorita, what's your name?"

"My name is Maria." And thus it had begun. Soon his friend had artfully disappeared, and Tomas was sitting on the towel beside her. She was staying with an aunt who had a house nearby, and he was camping just down the beach, he said. The time passed all too quickly for them. He told her of his aspirations to become an artist, a dancer.

"And you?" he asked. "What do you want to be?"

"It's not nearly so interesting," she said.

"Come now," Tomas said. "I'll bet you're a college girl. Smart girl like you."

She nodded.

"And what are you studying?"

"Paleontology."

"Ah!" Tomas said. "I love paleontology."

She laughed. "Do you even know what paleontology is?"

"Certainly. It is the study of…things which are pale."

It was September, but the warm weather lingered, and over the course of just a few days, Maria and Tomas became extremely close. It was clear that there was a very strong connection between them. They went for hikes on the woodland paths that encircled the lake, and on breezy mornings, they took out the little green sailboat that belonged to her aunt. On their last day, they went for a picnic on a deserted stretch of the lake. Off the shore, a pontoon dock was anchored to the bottom; boats could tie up to it, but today there was no one else around.

They swam out to the dock, hauled themselves up, and lay in the sun. After a time, without saying a word, Tomas rolled over and brought his lips down to hers. He had done it many times over these past few days, in this same way, suddenly, without speaking. The first time, she had been so nervous that she had forgotten to kiss back, but he was not easily discouraged, and she'd had many chances since then to correct her error.

This time, though, Tomas's hands were wandering where they shouldn't.

"Can't do that," Maria said, shoving his forearm.

"Come on," Tomas breathed. "I cannot believe you wouldn't trust me by now."

"No, it's too soon for that."

"Soon it will be too late. Summer is over, don't you see?" His hand began to move again along her thigh.

Finally she sat up and said, "No, Tomas. Maybe if we meet here again in a few weeks, and our feelings are still as strong, then maybe. But not now. We've only just met."

He sat up, too, and encircled his knees. "I'm sorry," he said. "I guess the girls I have known before now didn't care so much." He looked at her, his warm brown eyes drawing her in, so that for a moment, she wondered whether she were the one making the mistake. "I'll be happy to wait until you feel the time is right," he said.

She put her arm around his neck, and said, "Thanks." Then she kissed him quickly on the cheek, stood up and leaped into the water. He followed, and there they were, swimming together, no ties, no promises, full of anticipation, and unfettered by adult life.

That was the moment, Maria thought, placing the picture back on the desk. *That was the best time in our lives, out there in the water, right then, and we didn't even know it. How could we have lost all of that? I wish we had run off together, never gotten married, never bought this house. We've wasted so much time, but perhaps we can still start over..*

Maria's reverie was interrupted by a brisk knock at the front door. She jumped. "My God," she said. "Please,

God, don't let it be bad news." She pulled her robe close about her throat and hurried to answer it.

It was the sleepy-eyed man again, Officer Sanchez, looking even more disheveled. His car sat at the curb, its motor idling. There was someone else in the car, a dark-haired man with a moustache, and for a surreal moment, she thought that it was Tomas, until she saw the uniform.

"Yes?" she said.

He rubbed his bristly chin. "I'm sorry, Dr. Escobar, but I'm going to have to ask you to come back down to the station with me. Please go inside and get dressed."

"Why? Have you located the right hospital? Where is my husband?"

Now he looked very sad. "Please don't argue with me, Señora," he said.

"I'm not arguing, but I don't understand why you can't just take me to the hospital?"

The uniformed officer in the car opened his door halfway and started to get out, but Sanchez motioned wearily for him to stay put. Then he turned back to Maria.

"I'm sorry, Dr. Escobar. I find it necessary to place you under arrest for suspicion in the murder of Tomas Escobar."

The sun was just glancing over the rooftops of Valencia. The driver honked his horn, and the gate went up, and they pulled around to a back entrance of the police station. They remained in the car until the gate descended behind them, and then two more men came out of the door and conferred with Officer Sanchez. They nodded; he quickly signed some papers, and then the others took her away.

They took her down the hall, where she was "processed" – fingerprinted and photographed and asked to fill out forms. A female officer watched her expressionlessly as she changed into a turquoise-colored jumpsuit. Then she was taken across a courtyard to the adjacent city jail, ushered into an ancient, creaking elevator and taken upstairs to the women's ward, which appeared to be one large open cell. It was all concrete blocks, with a concrete floor, artificial lighting, cream-colored bars, and with one sink and one toilet in a stall with no door. The sound here echoed so that even the loudest voices were garbled and distorted, and over all hung a sickening smell of fried pork. Maria could feel the weight of the little clear-plastic bag of toiletries which someone had handed her, but otherwise she moved as if she were in a dream.

A guard directed her to a bunk built into the side of the wall, and she went over and sat down. She stared with amazement. There were women everywhere, perhaps forty or fifty in number, in their turquoise jumpers, some lying on their beds, some sitting, and others talking in small groups. Three big women stared at her silently. She peered up at the one-way mirror. She thought she could make out two people, probably two guards, on the catwalk above, thin and wavering, and practically obscured by the dirt and condensation on the mirror, two more shadow figures in the nightmare that would not end.

15

"I've got to get out of this house for a while," Sarah said to her husband. "Why don't we go camping this weekend?"

The two little race cars immediately started whirling around the house. They didn't camp often, but each one had his own camping bag with all the proper stuff – canteen, mess kit, and so on. It didn't take very long for them to be ready. They grabbed their bags, packed in some clothes, and chose some books and games to take along.

Mom and Dad took longer to get ready, but after about an hour, they got the car loaded, and off they went.

"Where are we going?" Ben asked.

"I think we should go to Anastasia Island," Sarah said.

"Where is that? Have we been there?"

"Sure, we have," Brad said. "Don't you remember? It's on the beach, in St. Augustine."

"We're going to the beach! Alex, the beach!" Ben yelled.

The older boy said nothing – he had already opened a book. He had been somewhat pensive since the stir over his mother had died down. Sarah knew there had been some teasing at school, but Alex seldom talked about such things; he had always been able to handle them on his own. She thought he would be all right, but had resolved to keep a close eye on him for a while.

"But when are we going to get there?" Ben insisted.

"You have a watch," Sarah said. "What time does it say right now?"

"I'm not sure. Alex, does this say nine?" He held up his wrist, and his brother nodded.

"So," Sarah said, "it should take about two hours from where we are now, so look at your watch, and when the big hand goes around two times, we should be there. What time will it be then?"

"Eleven," Ben said.

"Very good. Now, why don't you see how many different states you can find on the other cars' license plates."

Ben looked out the window, and soon both he and his brother were asleep.

In a soft voice, Sarah asked her husband, "Are you worried at all about Alex?"

Brad shook his head. "No, he'll be fine. He's been through a lot lately. I guess we all have."

"Believe me," she said. "I could never have imagined any of this happening."

"What's the latest news?" Brad asked.

"Nothing since they made the connection to that dinosaur DNA they found in Montana a few years ago."

"Yeah," Brad said. "I can definitely see a connection between you and a Tyrannosaurus Rex."

She lightly punched his shoulder. "The weird thing is, I *have* been around dinosaur remains before. Remember, I told you about that trip to China with my Dad, back when I was eighteen?"

"Sure. The one that got hit by a meteor. I mean, how unlucky is that? You're minding your own business, munching on some grass, and zap."

"Except that it probably wasn't grass. Probably it was another dinosaur. But those were all fossilized remains, no soft tissue like they found frozen in Montana."

Brad shrugged. "Search me. I almost failed biology in college."

She arranged the pillow she had brought against the passenger side window. Soon she was dozing, and her dreams took her to old places – her parents' house, her father's old office. Then she drifted away, and found herself in the desert again. Maria was there, leaning over the fossilized bones with a little whisk broom. She was talking excitedly. And then Mae Ling was there. She was holding up her arm to show Sarah something – it was blood, a dark streak running from her hand down along the curve of her elbow.

Sarah woke up, startled. "My God," she muttered. "I'd forgotten about that."

Brad looked over. "What's that, hon'?"

She shook her head groggily. "This girl that was on the camping trip with us to the Gobi Desert. She cut her hand. It bled quite a bit, all over some chicken we were cutting up."

"Gross," Brad said. "I hope she was all right."

"Oh, we wrapped it up and washed everything. She probably needed stitches, but we were way out in no-man's land. I've tried to get in touch with her, but she seems to have just disappeared."

"Well, it is China after all. Billions of people."

"I know," Sarah said. "It's just so weird how certain things and people keep coming back to me, since all of this started happening. Did I tell you I got in touch with Maria Escobar the other morning, the paleontologist who was on that same trip with us? "

"No. How did you manage that?"

"The magic of the internet. Her situation is just like mine."

"What do you mean?"

"She's immune. No sign of the virus."

Brad had learned to steer her away from this topic – it would only lead to sleep deprivation and further stress for everyone. "She was from Spain, right? I always wanted to go to Spain."

Sarah punched his arm again. "Okay, I get it. I'll shut up." She looked out the window, and saw the Bridge of Lions in rising into view. "Oh, wow. I didn't know we were this close. Where is this place again?"

"It's just over the bridge. See the lighthouse? The park is right there."

"Guess I better wake the kids up." "Do we go swimming right away?"

They turned at the lighthouse – it had been recently renovated and repainted, its white and black stripes gleaming in the mid-day sun. They drove up to the gate, paid for their spot, and picked it out on the map. After a short drive down a gravel road, past the surf school and into a pine grove, they pulled into their campsite.

Ben's sleepy voice emanated from the back seat: "Dad, can we go swimming?"

"Sure, but we have to set up camp first. If I remember correctly, the last time, we did it in eight minutes. Let's try and break our record."

Brad opened the trunk and tossed the two bags which held the dome tent out onto the ground. The boys removed the tarp, the stakes and poles, and the tent itself. Very quickly they had the poles through the slots on the tent, and the whole affair was lifted with very little effort.

"Throw me the stakes," Brad said. He went from spot to spot as they tossed each stake to him. He looped them through the lines, inserted them into the ground, and then stepped on them with his boot.

"Okay, Mom, we need your help," Brad said. The tarp went over everything, and their home for the night was up. Then they hauled out the cooler, put their backpacks inside the tent, set the lantern on the picnic table, and all was in readiness.

Ben cried out, "How fast? How fast did it take?"

"Seven minutes, forty seconds. That's it. It's a new world record."

Now both boys yelled and high-fived each other. "Can we go swimming now?"

"Sure," Brad said. "Get your bathing suits on."

Together they went along the trail that led down to the beach. It was nearly deserted, except for an older couple with their arms around one another. Ben and Alex ran out and leapt into the surf as their parents found a spot on the sand to put the big blanket on. Sarah looked over at her husband.

"I know you're tired of hearing about it," she said. "But I was just thinking…everything feels like we're starting all over again."

"That's good for our marriage, isn't it?"

"No, I don't mean just you and me. I mean…everything. It just feels like something is coming to an end, and something else is beginning."

Brad looked out at the ocean. "I think I know how you feel. Like everyone is expecting something of you."

"You're right. I've been thinking lately I'd like to go back to church."

"Okay," he said. "We will."

"I mean, I'm not sure what we're supposed to do, but I believe God is supposed to be a part of it. No, that's not right – I'm supposed to be a part of whatever it is that God has in mind. I guess that's what I mean."

"I'm with you," Brad said. "I mean, I'll follow your lead."

"I'm not a leader. I realized that a while back. I'm what they used to call a homemaker, a housewife."

"Nothing wrong with that."

"But it's all changing," she said.

"It has to."

She slipped her hand into his and put her head on his shoulder. "Thanks for understanding."

But that night, after they had eaten their camp dinner of beans and franks and had stared into the fire until they all grew so tired they could barely crawl into the tent, Sarah dreamed again of Mae Ling. This time she could see her face clearly – that sad expression she had assumed midway through their expedition. And then slowly, she lifted her arm again to reveal the dark blood which flowed along the back of it and trickled along the curve of her elbow. This time Sara walked toward her, touched the blood, and then examined her fingers.

She woke up suddenly. The tent was close and stuffy, and full of the sounds of breathing. She fished the flashlight out of her backpack, unzipped the tent, and went out into the darkness. She could feel that her heart was still racing. She skirted the edges of the campsite with her light until she found the trail, and she silently plunged in among the trees and palmetto shrubs.

It seemed farther than she remembered, and very dark. Maybe this wasn't such a good idea, after all. Her heart would not slow its pace. Something moved off to her left, and she shone the light on the tree trunks. About fifty yards away, a pair of yellow eyes gleamed back at her. She walked more quickly.

At last she reached the beach, a soft stretch of white. The sky was overcast, but the edges of morning were visible beyond the sea, a colorless but welcome light. She went to the water and waded in – it was warm. She dipped her hands in, then splashed her face, tasted the salt on her lips, and at last she began to feel calm again.

She looked up into the dark gray void. "What is it I'm supposed to do?" she asked aloud. She wasn't really sure whom she was speaking to: her father? Mae Ling? God? But it didn't matter; the only reply was the sound of the surf, the only sign the pale dawn as it broke once more over the suffering world.

16

An eye for an eye, was all Maria could think as she sat there, lonely, on her cot. She had begun to pass the hours thinking of ways to torture and pay back those who were now clearly responsible for the pain in her own life, and for Tomas's murder. Something was terribly wrong. She had convinced herself that her arrest was a set-up by those who had killed her husband. She had been here for five days now, had not seen a judge, had not spoken to an attorney – in fact, she had had no contact with anyone at all, except for brief exchanges with the guards when they brought the meals around. It was all so bizarre.

At first she had been overwhelmed by the loss of Tomas. Although they had led separate lives in so many ways, she now understood how much she had depended on him. Then, the more she had thought about things, the greater her sense of betrayal had become. She didn't know for sure who was involved, but she felt certain it was much bigger than a simple robbery or random act of violence. Nothing made sense. She resolved that no matter what happened, she would see things through and find out who was responsible for Tomas's demise. Restitution would be her mantra.

Still she was trapped within these concrete blocks. How was she going to get out of here? She knew that ultimately, she would have to have a hearing, and then a trial, if it came to that. Spanish law must provide a lawyer for her. But so far, she had been given no opportunity to contact anyone on the outside, and she was surprised that no one from her department at the university, with whom she had kept in contact by email, had come searching for her. Even worse, she didn't know her true circumstances, and she had no idea what would come in the near future. Every time the rough-looking women stared at her, she looked away, but she knew she could not continue to avoid them. Her moment of reckoning was coming.

The women's jail had its problem, but mostly it was in the form of abuse by the men who ran the facility. She had overheard some of the women telling horrific stories of having been forced to have sex with certain guards, and she had observed how, in general, many of the women seemed to console and care for one another here. Still, she kept to herself, and waited.

At last, on her sixth morning, a guard on the catwalk above called down: "Escobar! Door Three!" She glanced around; several women gawked at her. She stood up, walked to the metal door, and stood there. The bolts tumbled, the door slid open, and she walked through. Another guard – a burly, hairy man – led her down the corridor to a dreary office with a cheap card table and two chairs. When he closed the door behind them, put his hands on his hips and grinned at her, her heart began to pound.

At that moment, a trim, gray-haired man in a three-piece suit and glinting spectacles entered the room. He set a bulging briefcase on the table and addressed the guard: "Leave us, please." The guard nodded and ducked out quickly. The man slid his glasses down his nose and looked at her. "Dr. Escobar? Please sit down."

He gazed at her intently for a moment across the table. Then he said, "My name is Eduardo Alvarez. I've been appointed by the Valencia courts to act as your attorney. Are you completely aware of the reason you're being held here?"

"Not really," she said. "I suppose they think I murdered my husband."

"Quite correct. But you had nothing to do with it, is that right?"

"Absolutely not," she said. "I love Tomas very much. I mean, I loved him. I'm sorry, I'm…just not myself right now."

"I understand, of course."

"Do you? I really *don't* understand any of this. I don't know why any of this is happening."

"Well," he said, pushing his spectacles back up again, "it's somewhat more complicated than I had thought, when I first opened your file. There are some things in here" – he pointed to his briefcase – "which make no sense at all to me either. That's why I had to meet with you right away."

"Right away? I've been in here for six days. Just going to the bathroom is a nightmare."

"Yes, well, the system moves slowly, you see. My apologies. In any case, why don't you explain to me exactly what happened on the night your husband was attacked."

She went through the whole story again. Even though her account was brief, since she had not seen much on that night, it was laborious to tell. Afterward, Alvarez sat with his fingertips together, studying her.

"Yes," he said. "It's all very strange."

"Can you tell me what's really going on?" Maria asked.

"There could be many answers to that."

She began to feel frustrated. "Then perhaps you can tell me why anyone would want to hurt Tomas. He was a professional entertainer. He only brought people pleasure."

Alvarez cleared his throat. "Yes, well, I offer you my deepest condolences for your loss. But the truth is, Dr. Escobar, there may have been certain aspects of your husband's…private affairs…of which you were unaware."

She glared at him. "Impossible. Tomas was an egotist, and sometimes very childish, but he kept no secrets from me. He was like an open book."

"I'm sure you're right. That part is of no consequence to us right now, anyway. What we must do is focus on securing your release, so that we can begin building your defense and examining all of the various angles. I'm afraid the court has not set bond for you yet, due to the seriousness of the charge. But I intend to devote my full attention to pursuing a bond hearing for you."

"I would appreciate that," she said. "I'm sure you're aware that I'm employed by the university. I'm a professor of paleontology. Perhaps you can call on my department head to provide a character reference."

Alvarez cleared his throat again and dug at his collar. "That's another aspect of this. I'm afraid that public opinion is not entirely on your side at the moment, Dr. Escobar. The university has officially offered no comment on your present circumstance."

"I haven't seen a newspaper at all. I've had no word. Has all of this been in the news?"

"Very much so. As you know, Tomas was a celebrity, and you have some notoriety of your own, given your status in the academic community. Also, the American media has made mention of your immunity."

"Immunity? I don't understand. How can I be in jail if I have immunity?"

"I mean your immunity to the virus. To Negra 9."

She was stunned. "But my medical records are private. No one has a right to that information."

"That may be. Nonetheless, it now seems to be public knowledge. And while we might think such a revelation would work in your favor, in fact, there has been a backlash."

"Backlash?"

"Yes. There is widespread resentment over the possibility of special treatment in your case."

"Special treatment?" Her voice grew louder. "Have you looked around this place? Besides, there are lots of women in Spain who are as healthy as I am."

"So we are told," Alvarez said. "In any case, my frank opinion is that we have quite a battle ahead of us. I'll do everything I can to help you." His look was quite genuine, even kind, fatherly. He was a good deal older than Maria, but she thought that he was not a bad-looking man – not as handsome as Tomas, of course, but…distinguished.

"One last thing," he said. "Have you ever heard of a Dr. Haman?"

"I don't recognize the name," she said. "Who is he?"

"He *was* a practicing gynecologist here in Valencia. But I am afraid he is no longer among us. Another homicide, the day after your husband. I'm just trying to cover all the possibilities."

"I'm afraid I didn't know him."

"Mm," Alvarez said. "Violent world we live in." He stood up and extended his hand.

"Thank you for coming," she said. "I hope to hear from you soon.

"You will. Don't lose hope."

17

Late in the afternoon, Sarah sat on the beach again, looking out over the wispy blue waters, the waves rolling, on and on, the water and sky, and the two boys' slender figures as they dove in and out of the surf. *How ridiculous that anyone might not believe in God*, she thought, *when these gifts are all around us.* She suddenly remembered a poem from her sophomore English class: it was by Robert Frost, something about not being able to look 'out far nor in deep' when you look at the sea. It's mostly mystery.

"Yet it's all around us," she said.

"What's that?" her husband said.

"Did I say something?" she asked.

"I'm sorry. I thought you did."

"Maybe I did. I was just thinking that every gift comes from God. With all that's going on, I wish I could focus on that more."

Brad lifted his beer to his lips, drank, and looked at his bottle. "I see what you mean – the ocean, the sun, the beer…"

"I was being serious," she said.

"Oh, me, too. The ocean, the beer, the girls…"

"Sorry, but the only girl here you should be noticing is me," she said.

"Well, yeah. That's what I meant." He smiled up at her.

"Are you all right?" she said. "Maybe you need to get out of the sun for a while."

"Nope. Gonna sit here all day."

"I thought so," she said.

Off to their left, two young couples, probably high-schoolers, were playing volleyball. It looked as if they were having a good time, and Sarah was watching them. One of the boys, who was getting ready to serve, took several steps forward behind the girl in front of him and grabbed the string at the top of her bathing suit and yanked it so the strings went flying, and the bathing suit went flying forward; she immediately grabbed it and pulled it back up. She turned around, and gave him a look, but said nothing.

"Did you see that?" Sarah said.

"See what?"

"That kid. He just went up and ripped off the top of that girl's bathing suit."

"And I missed it?"

"Brad," she said. "You know my father would have killed you if he'd seen you do something like that to me. That's just not right. Why didn't she get mad?"

"Sorry," he said. "You're right. It's not funny. I hope that Ben and Alex will know better than to act that way."

"Well, we have to teach them." He nodded.

"When it comes down to it," she continued, "nothing is harmless. Everything matters. The littlest things, things you'd never expect to matter – they do."

"I'm with you, hon'," Brad said. "It's like running red lights. Some people occasionally run a yellow light, feel bad about it, and try not to do it again. Other people see a yellow light, and they speed up. Gets worse every day, but I suspect there was a time when everyone knew the yellow meant slow down. And there it is: we've got to get back to a world that slows down on yellow, stops on red."

"What are you talking about?" Sarah said.

"You didn't get my metaphor?"

"You're a goofball. We need to go get the steaks ready for dinner. The kids are probably turning into prunes, anyway."

"Okay," he said. "Give me about a half-hour, bring the kids up, and then we'll eat."

"Sounds fine," she said. He walked away up the sand, and she turned her eyes back to the sea, though she could see neither out far nor in deep.

18

It was lunchtime on day seven, and Maria went down, got in line, and got her plate. As had become her way, she did not speak nor look directly at anyone all the way through the line. She went to a table by herself and sat down. But something different happened this time: a young, dark-haired girl carried her tray over, smiled at her, and said, "May I?"

Maria said nothing, but gestured to an empty chair. The girl was a brand-new inmate. That was nothing unusual – inmates arrived every day, and in general it was like a big, ongoing reunion for them. But this girl, like Maria, had kept to herself.

"Thanks. My name is Arabella." She stuck out a small hand.

"I'm Maria."

"I know who you are. You've been all over the news."

"Have I?"

"Killing your husband attracts a lot of press, especially when he's semi-famous."

"I didn't kill my husband."

"Hey, I'm not an attorney, and I'm certainly not a judge. I'm just telling you what they're saying on TV and in the papers about you. That and your immunity to the virus. That's why I came to sit with you. I'm the same as you."

"Same as me?"

Arabella nodded, looked about her, then whispered, "I can't catch it either. The doctors can't figure out why."

"I don't see why that should be any of my business," Maria said, turning back to her food.

"Don't you see what's going on here?" the girl asked. "Why don't you think any of them – the other women in here – why don't you think they've bothered you, or even talked to you? They think you've got some sort of power. In some jails I've been in, the prisoners divide themselves up by race, skin color, or in some places by gang affiliation. In here, these days, it's those who have the virus and those who don't."

"Do you mean to tell me that I'm the only one in here that doesn't have the Negra 9 virus?"

"Well, you were the only one, but now I'm here, too. And I don't plan on getting infected."

"But nobody knows how the disease is passed."

Arabella put a spoonful of noodles in her mouth. "Blood," she said. "Blood-borne pathogen. Needles. Or sexual contact, and I'm not up for either one."

"Then I guess we do have that much in common," Maria said. "But how do you know when someone else has it? I mean, it's not like measles."

"It's not hard. Did you get tampons in your little plastic bag?" Maria nodded. "Well, they didn't," Arabella said, gesturing towards the women who were lined up for food.

"Why are you in here?"

"Oh, I just took a few things that didn't belong to me…but let's not talk about that right now. We're just two girls having a little lunch."

Maria smiled. "Okay," she said, and turned back to the tasteless globs in front of her. At once, she felt dizzy, set down her fork, and leaned her forehead against her palm.

"What's the matter?" asked Arabella.

"I don't know. I'm just very tired. I can't sleep in here. I've got to get out."

"We all want to get out."

"No, I mean I really have got to get out of here. I haven't committed any crime, but I just think that someone here is out to get me."

"Sounds like some type of science fiction novel or something. Maybe you're just being paranoid." Arabella lowered her voice to a mock spooky tone: "Or maybe they want our eggs... Yes, we are the egg women... They want to breed us with aliens. Wait a second – that might be sort of fun."

"Oh, stop that," Maria said. "I couldn't be more serious about this. If I stay here, I'll die." She looked over at the group of tough-looking women who always seemed to be staring back at her.

"Don't worry about them," Arabella said. "I'm here now. We can look after one another."

So they did. Through some negotiations to which Maria was not privy, Arabella procured the bunk next to hers, and they became constant companions. She was from Madrid, originally, and her world had been entirely different from Maria's, but she was smart and streetwise. She had many brothers and sisters and cousins and uncles and aunts, she said, but she had always been the proverbial black sheep. Only one other besides her, her brother

Rafael, had ever been in trouble with the law. "But he's still a very good boy," she said. There were whispered stories from her in the dark hours, wild tales of liquor and men and the bars and cafes of Madrid, for which Maria had no chapters of her own to add. She realized that in spite of all her work in the university, and in spite of the semi-public life she had led as Tomas's wife, she really did not know very much at all.

One week after Arabella's arrival, she found that the girl could not get out of bed in the morning. She looked quite pale, and she had curled herself into a tight ball beside the concrete blocks. Maria placed a hand on her forehead. "You're burning up," she said. "I'm going to call a guard."

"Don't," Arabella groaned. "It's just cramps. I'm starting my period, I think. Just leave me."

But Maria would not leave her, missing breakfast and lunch, swabbing Arabella's head and neck with a damp cloth from time to time as the girl drifted in and out of a fitful sleep throughout the day. Late in the afternoon, she said, "Arabella, you should try to drink something. I'll get some water."

"I can't. My stomach hurts. My head hurts."

Maria felt her cheek again – she was even warmer now, and she was very pale about her lips. "Listen, I don't care what you say, I'm calling a guard. This is not just pre-menstrual cramps."

When they were putting Arabella on a gurney and preparing to take her upstairs to the clinic, she had looked over at Maria and smiled. Then she gestured for her to come near. Maria put her ear to the girl's lips.

"Rafael Martinez," whispered Arabella. "He lives on Via Primera, but you'll usually find him at a café called El Presidente."

"I'm afraid I don't understand," Maria said.

"My brother Rafael, the one I told you about. If you ever do get out, he can help you. The café is called El Presidente. He works there." Before Maria could respond, the guards had briskly wheeled her away, and the girl had looked back once and smiled.

Now Maria sat on the edge of her bunk, her head in her hands. What would she do now? For the first time, the grimness of her situation, the true hopelessness of it, fell upon her like a fog, and she felt her heart sinking, down, down. *What's going to happen to me,* she thought. *Tomas, how could you let this happen?*

When the young girl from Madrid returned two days later, she went to her bunk but did not speak to her. Maria sat up. "Thank God!" she said. "You're back! I thought you were really sick. I thought you'd be gone for a long time. Are you all right?"

Arabella had begun folding up her blanket and collecting her things. She still did not speak. Now Maria stood up.

"Are you being released? Did your family post bail?" No reply. "Something's wrong," Maria said. "Arabella, what is it? What have I done?"

The girl turned to her. Her face was utterly void of any emotion. "You haven't done anything. It's just how it is in here. I can't talk to you anymore. I'm one of them." She nodded toward the group of girls who were seated around a table, disinterestedly playing a game of cards.

Maria stared at her pleadingly, and touched her arm. "It doesn't matter! I swear, it doesn't!"

"Of course, it does." Arabella zipped the little bag of personal items.

"Please don't leave me!" Maria cried. "Oh, this is terrible!"

"Terrible?" Arabella said coldly. "What could you possible know about it?" And with that, she wandered away into the crowd of inmates who were milling about.

Maria lay in her bunk for a long time, shielding her eyes from the fluorescent light which cast no shadow. The hours passed, women went to supper, returned, went to shower, returned. At last, the guard on the walkway above crossed from one side to the other – the signal for them to get into their bunks – and the lights went off. She was not sure whether she slept, but at some point, an idea seemed to unfold itself in her brain. She opened her eyes to the darkness.

So simple. I'll tell them I'm sick. Just like Arabella. Of course, when they get me up to the clinic and take my blood and run their little tests, they'll know it's not true, but at least I'll be out of here. At least I'll have some sort of chance. Maybe there's a window. Maybe I could run. She felt her will returning to her. *Maybe I could get away.*

Morning arrived soon, the fluorescent lights came back on, and the other inmates began to stir all about her. Within, she steeled herself, but without, she tried to will

herself to look weak, sick, pale. She curled herself into a
ball and faced the wall, and waited. An hour passed, and
she heard the male guard's voice beside her bunk.

"Escobar?" She said nothing, but groaned a little.
"Escobar! Get your lazy ass out of that bunk. Your lawyer
is here to see you. Door Three."

Sheepishly, she rose, put on her slippers, and went
to the sink and brushed her teeth. As she crossed the rec
area, she felt the eyes of the other women on her, and she
searched for Arabella's face in the crowd. There she was –
their eyes met for an instant, and then the girl turned her
back to her.

The tumblers moved, the big door slid open, and the
guard escorted her down the corridor. This time he did not
enter the room at all, but only opened the door and
motioned for her to go in.

Eduardo Alvarez was seated at the table, glasses
perched on the end of his nose; he was making notes on a
pad of legal paper. He wore a blue three-piece today and a
gray and pink paisley tie, and without looking up or saying
a word, he motioned with his pen for her to take the seat
opposite him. He continued scribbling away. At last he

looked up at her, removed a file from his briefcase, and said, "I have some papers for you to sign."

"Oh, no," she said. "Please, no more forms. What are they?" she asked.

"Release forms. Seems a friend has posted bail for you. You're getting out today."

It had been seventeen days, but when she walked out into the bright morning sunlight and saw the busy streets of Valencia, alive with color, the noise of traffic, and the smells of pastry and good coffee coming from the cafes, Maria was sure that she was ten years older than when she had entered this place.

"Come along," Eduardo said, "I'll give you a lift."

As they drove along La Gran Via, and she felt her life, her real life, creeping back into her veins, her very fingers, she turned to him. "I – I don't know what to say," she said. "I don't know how to thank you."

It had been Alvarez himself who had posted her bail – all 200,000 Euros – though he had put everything in his brother's name, officially. It was Alvarez who had been tirelessly insisting, for days on end, on a bail hearing for her, and who had appeared on her behalf before the judge. It was Alvarez who had pled her case ("Look, this woman is no threat to anyone. She's a dignified and respected scientist, a professor. And she's absolutely no threat to run away. I will personally vouch for her character and for her appearance at trial in six months...")

"No thanks necessary," he said, "but I will make a suggestion." He stared intently at the car in front of him and cleared his throat. "Please don't take this the wrong way. I'd like you to come and stay at my apartment for a time. I have an extra room with a private bath downstairs – my daughter is away at school right now. I've gotten wind of a few things... I just think it would be safer for you there, for the foreseeable future, than at your house."

She could not help the slight smile, and she turned her face away shyly. "I didn't think lawyers were supposed to get personally involved with their clients."

"Trust me," he said. "It's not personal. It's just much safer. The suspicions you expressed about your husband's death...I think there's credibility there."

Now she looked at him. His face was quite stoic. "All right," she said. "I will."

"Very good. Are you hungry?"

She was, in fact, starving.

Mae Ling gazed out of her hotel window to the brightly lit, traffic-clogged streets below. So this was New York – it was more or less as she had imagined it would be: a very tall place, even a little frightening, but humming with life and vigor. And unlike the cities she knew in China, it never closed...she wondered if people ever rested here.

Her hotel was decent, not fancy by any means, but well within her budget. She was stretching the money her father had left her as best she could, and found that she could be quite thrifty: no restaurants (the big sandwich carts on the streets here were sufficient for her, if somewhat unremarkable), no movies (she did love to go to the cinema, though, and would have to indulge herself at some point). Despite the vibrancy of her surroundings, she was still quite tired, and hoped to rest here for at least one more day before continuing her journey, so there would be the hotel bill of another night, but she regarded a decent bed with clean sheets as part of her rehabilitative therapy. Tomorrow she must look at train and bus schedules to

Florida – she thought she could save a little that way, instead of flying. Besides, she was used to that sort of travel – no one in China took domestic flights.

She went back to the little writing desk and looked again at the papers she had spread out there. There was a map of the U.S., and the worn *National Geographic* magazine with the obituary for John Pippins, where she had circled "Lake City, Florida," in red, and the photo of her father which had also been in the box behind the old house in Jining. She had been keeping a journal, as well, in order to practice her writing in English. She looked over her notes on her trip up to this point:

Echeng

(4 pm) The bus ride from Jining to Echeng is beautiful, though perhaps this is only because I know that I am actually escaping at last. But it is a rugged, wonderful countryside which I had the good fortune to see once before, when I was with the travel agency. There are many times now when I wish I had bought a camera. Still, the images I have stored in my memory are vivid: fields of greens, fruits, and peanuts; horse-drawn wagons; tall pine

trees: ancient stone houses with blue tile roofs. I remember well these farmers along the road, carrying hay bundles on their backs and shoulders, as they have done for centuries, no doubt. The crops are primarily grown along the riverbeds, and water buffalo still pull the old ploughs, and there are haystacks built around trees in the shapes of hats. And as always, there are the mountains, their peaks growing ever sharper in the clean light.

(8 am the following day) My time in Echeng was brief, to say the least. I arrived around 11:00 pm. But there were many people outside the bus station, family members waiting, and a few merchants. Despite the late hour, I managed to secure accommodations for the night, a small room with dirty walls and carpets, but certainly no worse than the place in Jining in which I had been living. I put my sleeping bag on the bed, crawled in, and slept soundly. Must make the bus by 8:15.

Jinan

(arrived 7pm) The journey from Echeng to Jinan was very long and hard, but without incident. It seems that just about every imaginable crop is grown in the Shandong

Province. It is uplifting to see such a bounty, and I suppose I am fortunate to be traveling in the summertime.

Still, like Jining and other places where I have been here, the town itself is dirty, with much rundown housing. The streets are lined with gnarled trees, but it almost seems that the exhaust and noise of the automobiles have choked them, so that they cannot bloom.

My room here is a bit better than the last – a very small hotel with a garden right outside my window, which makes the dirty room seem a little nicer. Accommodations are not as cheap here, as I had to pay 137 Yuans for tonight. Still, I need a bed – I find that I am still craving sleep.

I did take time for a short walking tour of the town, and ate in a local market run by a man who agreed to practice English with me. I had fried vegetables and a watery soup, but at least I was full.

Tiajin

(7 am) During the bus ride, I tried to relax, but did not have much success, as Beijing looms ever more near. We crossed the river many times on massive bridges, drove

on superhighways the whole time, and saw many modern factories, hotels, resorts, and shopping centers. When we entered the Special Economic Zone, a few people got off the bus, but I remained aboard and tried to nap, again without much luck.

When we rolled into Tiajin last evening, I was shocked by the size of the town. I was here once as a girl, but so much has changed.

I had to walk quite some distance to find a place to stay for the night. The first hotels I encountered were either filled up or were too expensive for me. My pack seemed to be growing heavier on my shoulders by the minute, and I was ready to find an alleyway in which to bed down for the night, but at every corner were prostitutes, grotesques, with their faces like heavily made-up skulls, and strange men who looked at me beneath their lowered hat brims, and I kept walking. At last I found an affordable room, though the desk clerk eyed me suspiciously. Noises came up to me from the streets below – not good sounds, but at last I slept.

This morning, the bus again, and then Beijing.

Beijing

(midnight) I don't know whether I can truly capture all of my excitement on paper. I have been in Beijing for three days now – a place I have been before, but never under such uncertain circumstances – trying to secure the proper forms and to purchase an airline ticket. Whatever they may write in the news, it is still very difficult for a Chinese citizen – especially a woman – to leave her own country. Now I know what my father was speaking of when he would complain about China's great bureaucracy.

The city is fairly deserted at this hour, except – oddly – for a few banks. There is a peculiar feeling of anti-climax here which I attribute to last year's Olympic Games. It is as if there was so much preparation, so much anticipation, and yet people on the streets now seem to look at one another as if to say, "Now what shall we do?"

I see that the Games changed Beijing in many ways, perhaps not all of them for the best. Many of the little markets and souvenir stands which had apparently sprung up like new buds have been shuttered. Sadly, old men sit on benches outside the restaurants, and their faces tell that they are wondering what has happened to all the people. I have read that our country did very well in the competition, and made great political gains in the world. But I cannot say that I think the average Chinese citizen's existence has been improved. Beijing is for the most part still a large city with the same problems – overcrowding, pollution, prostitution...

I approached the offices of the Chinese International Travel Service with some trepidation, and rightly so. I have learned that they will not hesitate to lie – I have spent hours on end filling out applications and forms, various formalities, and each time they hand me something new. But I think my will is stronger than theirs – I return again tomorrow to see what sort of new troubles they have in store for me. In the meantime, I was able to secure reasonable accommodations in a clean, safe hotel, in a good location. Overall, I think my luck has been very good on this journey.

My first night in the city was the least pleasant. Even though it is summer now, Beijing gets chilly at night. I had on two layers of clothing, but my knit gloves with holes in them and my old shoes were not the best things to be wearing. I headed down one of the main avenues and ended up in an expensive shopping area. I somehow worked my way back to the Chinese Art Gallery, where I saw images of the country – the China of my childhood - which I shall always remember. I was directly behind the Forbidden City, in an area called Old Beijing, with a walled neighborhood of traditional houses. Across the street from the art gallery, I had dinner at a noodle shop with wonderful fried rice and decent prices. The food in Beijing has been pretty good, and I have not seen any floating pigeon heads – which I never liked.

My second day, after being frustrated once again at the travel service offices, I decided to treat myself to a cheap tourist's bus to the Great Wall at Mutianyu. My father took me there when I was ten, and those memories came back to me in a sudden and bittersweet stream. The drive there was lovely – all of the streets were lined with trees. Most people get around Mutianyu by bicycle, but there are also pretty horse-drawn carriages, and a steady flow of cars – lots of American cars, particularly Jeep Cherokees. I had about two hours to climb around on the Great Wall, and I must say that once again I felt that my father was with me – not the man of fourteen years ago, but his spirit as it is now – alive, happy, and comforting. I am very proud to have been there once again as a Chinese citizen, especially since I do not truly know when I shall be

*in my homeland again (provided I can sort out my troubles
with the international travel service).*

*My ride back to the city was equally moving. The
terrain was a strange mix of rural, suburban, and urban.
The road was broad like a highway, but not much has been
built in the area. There were perhaps two towns along the
way, a half-dozen factories, and a handful of shepherds
with their flocks: they stood by the road and stared as we
passed – watchers from another century.*

*My third day in Beijing – today – was a hectic one.
I had a wonderful hot shower, and did some laundry, and
started into the city feeling very hopeful. I took my usual
route on the 103 bus, headed towards the travel office. Yet
again, I was turned away with a new handful of
requirements and special forms, mostly involving my
family's history. On my way back, I decided to stop at
Tiananmen Square. I entered from the back of the square,
so that I could see how large it truly is. I then crossed the
street, and worked my way past the Forbidden City. An
American couple approached me, and the husband asked if
he could take a photo of his wife with me in front of the
great palace. I nearly laughed – I remembered what the
man from the tour guide company in Jining said to me so*

*many years ago – I have the sort of face Westerners expect
to see in China. I'm still not sure what that means.*

*As for tonight, an inexpensive dinner once again at
the noodle house across the street has left me feeling full
and almost happy again. Now ... back to the paperwork.*

Air China Flight 203: somewhere over the Yellow Sea

*(2:10 pm) Once it happened, it happened quickly.
The international travel service finally declared me eligible
for passage, but even up to the moment when I handed my
ticket and boarding pass to the agent at the counter, it was
as if no one wished me to go. This I will never understand.
Why do they care? My life is small. What is it truly worth?*

*In any case, I am here, and on my way, rising,
rising. But I am not afraid – I hear my father's voice.*

And now, here she was. Little Mae Ling in the
biggest, most populous, most cosmopolitan city on earth.
She picked up her pen and made a new entry:

New York City

(11 pm) It has been an arduous journey, but it is far from over.

My luck holds, as I was again able to find clean accommodations at a reasonable price. There is a market on the corner of the block where my hotel is, a Chinese market. Foolishly, I went in and immediately walked to the counter, where a middle-aged woman with graying hair was reading a Chinese newspaper – it was the Beijing Daily News*! I greeted her in our native tongue, and she didn't even look up at first.*

"Hello," I said again. "I've just arrived from the homeland. I – I came in to…I don't know why I came in." I was about to turn away. "I suppose I am just a little too excited." I muttered.

"Wait," she said. I stopped. "What province are you from?" It was my own dialect.

"Shandong," I said.

"I am also from Shandong," she said.

"I know," I said.

We chatted for perhaps ten minutes. I told her all about my troubles getting out of Beijing, and she nodded in agreement; I told her about my home in Jining, and she said, "Yes, I know the town well"; I told her about my flight and my intention to take the bus for Florida tomorrow.

"That's a very long way," she said. "I have a sister who lives in Orlando, if you happen to go there as well. I'll write her number down for you." She did so.

At last, a customer came in, and I said. "Well, I suppose I should get some rest. Thank you for your kindness."

She smiled, and then she spoke in English: "Welcome to America, and good luck."

"Thanks," I said. "It's hard for me to believe I'm really here."

It *was* difficult to believe, and Mae Ling got up and went over to the window again just to prove to herself that it was really true.

This time she noticed something odd: there were two men parked in front of the building, in a shiny Honda. The driver was clearly looking up directly at her window. The other man was standing outside the passenger door, also looking up with what seemed to be a small pair of binoculars. There was nothing particularly unusual about their appearance – both wore casual collared shirts. She stared back at them, and the man who was standing got quickly back into the car, and the driver rolled his window up and pulled out into the stream of traffic.

She was startled, and when she'd had a few moments to think about it, quite frightened. Then, a half-hour or so later, she was uncertain of what she had actually seen. Had they really been looking at her window, or perhaps the one above? Had those really been binoculars, or had the man simply been shielding his eyes against the streetlight?

She got into bed, and pulled the crisp sheets up to her chin. She resolved to try and forget about what she thought she had seen. Still, it was a long time before she went to sleep.

Even when she saw them again the following morning, on her way to the subway, she tried to convince herself that it was a coincidence. But there they were, same dark-haired men in the same blue Honda, rolling slowly along, both of them gawking at her unabashedly. Her heart began to thump, and she quickened her pace.

She did not realize at first that it was a pawn shop she had ducked into – she had just seen the big yellow sign, the big store clerk through the cluttered window, and she had made a sharp right turn and entered the shop.

Pawn shop. No such thing back in Jining. As she calmed down again, she walked the narrow aisles, looked around at the stereos, the televisions, the DVD players, many with little stickers proclaiming, "Made in China." Then, as she made her way back toward the front of the store, she noticed the handguns lined up in the glass counter – sinister, gleaming, beckoning. The baldheaded man behind the counter, whose shoulders seemed as broad as the counter was long, looked up at her. "Help you?" he said.

She pointed at a small silver one with a white handle. "How much for that one?" she asked.

"That .22 right there? I can let it go for a hunnerd."

Impulsively, she began to fish through her bag for her cash, but the clerk said, "Hey, whoa, wait a minute, now. I can't just sell it to you. You gotta fill out some forms. You gotta go down to the local precinct and get an application. No exceptions."

"How long does all that take?" she asked.

"'Bout six months," the clerk said.

"Oh," she said. Never mind, then." Then her gaze fell upon a bone-handled knife on a red velvet cloth. "What about that?"

"That? Four-inch hunting knife. No permit necessary. Fifty bucks."

"I'll take it," she said.

At least it was something. More than she had before anyway. She looked about for the blue car, but it was nowhere to be seen. She hurried along toward the subway stairwell, feeling the added weight of the bone and steel in her bag as it swung against her side.

20

Brad's parents had come to stay for a few days. One night they offered to watch the kids and he and Sarah went out to eat – a rare treat for them.

The two of them were in the car, on their way to their favorite Italian place, and Brad held Sarah's hand as he drove.

> He said, "Do you still remember how we met? I remember like it was yesterday. It was at the Willie Nelson concert in Gainesville. I had a big blanket spread out, and you came over to me, begging to share mine because you had nowhere to sit. With every song Willie sang, you kept inching closer to me, and closer to me. By the time he got to 'You Were Always on My Mind,' you were touching me, and I knew for certain that you liked me. Even after the concert was over, and people were leaving, we just sat there talking for hours. Finally, they had to kick us out. We went and sat in the back of my pick-up, looking up at the stars and talking. You asked for my phone number. You wouldn't quit hounding me, so I promised to take you out the next night."

"*Hounding you*?" Sarah said. "Okay, that's a pretty accurate recollection, except for just a few really small details. We went to see the university orchestra play a starlight concert that night. *I* had a large blanket with some folding chairs, and a complete spread of wine, cheese, crackers, and grapes. It was a small get-together with my roommates. One of them didn't feel well, and so the other one agreed to take her home, but I wanted to stay for the music. You, seeing an opportunity for free food and the last remaining spot close to the stage, decided to barge in. You plopped down on the blanket next to me, and I said 'excuse you.' You turned and looked at me and said, 'Oh! I'm so sorry, I mistook you for someone else.' You were miserable at lying, and finally you had to confess that you indeed knew you didn't belong there, didn't know me, and shouldn't have been sitting there. Then you tried to claim that your love of Mozart had driven you to do it. Unfortunately, they were playing Haydn that night.

"When the concert was over, and you were walking with me to the parking lot, it was very dark. But for some reason, I had started to trust you, and I let you walk me to my car. Lucky for you, you didn't try any funny business that night, but you relentlessly *hounded* me for the rest of the week, calling me at least three times every day. Finally, I agreed to go out with you because you had worn down my will to say no."

"And we went to the Willie Nelson concert, right?"

"Yes, Brad. We went to the Willie Nelson concert."

"See?" he said. "I knew I had it right."

21

The *Passion,* a scrap metal tanker out of Antwerp and weighing in at 7,800 deadweight tons and flying under the flag of Panama, nosed into the broad Atlantic at 10 knots, bound for Miami.

Dr. Maria Escobar was tucked safely away in quarters adjacent to Captain Leigh's cabin, although "safely" was probably not the word she would have chosen. If she had been disturbed by the packs of inmates in the general population cell in Valencia's jail, here she suffered the pangs of solitary confinement. If she had been trying to find a place in which to be safe and secure, certainly she would not have opted for a rusty ship in the middle of the ocean with a bunch of men for three weeks, even if they were not aware of her presence. Captain Leigh, a nice enough man, had told her to "sit tight" in the little room with metal walls, but she was tired of being in jail; besides, it was late, and very dark, from what she could see from her tiny porthole. She was desperate to get out on deck.

Only a few weeks ago, she could never have dreamed that her life would become one of such loneliness and dismay, that she would come to know concrete and metal so well, or be forced into hiding like a hunted animal. When she had gone to the home of the attorney, Eduardo Alvarez, she had felt as if she had a chance at reprieve: things had gone well at first – they talked at length almost every evening about her case, about the approach they would take at her trial next December, as she wracked her brain time and again, albeit painfully, about that strange evening of Tomas's death. It seemed so long ago, what had happened there on the balcony of their home in Valencia. The voices she had heard, her last glimpse of Tomas lying there, shirtless, still slender, still beautiful, and the sequence of odd events later on at the police station and back at home. It still seemed all so senseless.

Then, she had made a terrible mistake…perhaps her only real crime, or at the very least, her only sin through all of this. One evening, during her third week of convalescence at Eduardo's apartment, he had come back rather late from his work, and Maria had prepared a good dinner of grilled fish and fresh vegetables. They had developed an interim domestic system which had so far worked very well, whereby he did the shopping, she did the cooking, and they shared all other chores. This way, she was able to stay indoors as much as possible, except when she took a book and went down to the little communal pool. There was hardly ever anyone there, and besides, the sun was part of her healing. In any case, the dinner was ready and waiting, but because of the hour, Maria had forgotten herself in consuming a bit too much wine. This was no excuse, she realized, for what happened later, but she had learned lately that, truly, nothing is meaningless, and nothing is without consequence.

So, the wine, the meal, the late hour, the way Eduardo looked at her so intently, as if he were actually seeing into her mind…whatever the combined reasons were, the result was singular: she had slept with Eduardo Alvarez that night. She could not even say she had "allowed" him to have her, for he had seemed as uncertain about it all as she, and he looked up at her several times during it all as if to say, "We should stop…we should talk…we should…" But soon it was too late for should. There was only the cold light of morning, and once he had showered, dressed, and gone out, there was the emptiness of the apartment.

Guilt had descended upon her, gripped her throat like a noose. Although in her youth she had been lighthearted, even flirtatious, she had only ever been with one other man, and that was Tomas. And even though Tomas was gone now, she was certain in her heart that she had betrayed him nonetheless. She gazed about Eduardo's bedroom, at the open closet with the blue suits, the ties, the shined shoes, the stacks of files, the little picture of his daughter, and it was all unknown to her. It was not her life. She must get out.

She sat down at his desk and tried several times to write him a letter, but everything she put down on paper seemed to be the hollow words of a hypocrite and a sinner who could not admit the truth of her sin. At last, she had settled on a brief note:

Dear Eduardo,

I hope you can forgive the transgressions of last night. It was not something I wanted to happen, nor was it something I had planned. But I find that I can no longer stay here, for many reasons. Someday I will repay you for all that you have done for me. You are a

very good man.

Yours in undying friendship,

Maria

Still inadequate, still terribly hollow, but it was the best she could do for now.

She turned to the computer, went online, and found the train tables for Madrid. She could be on the Renfe express in one hour; she quickly packed her things – the few things she had left – in her tweed suitcase, made sure she had the cash that she had taken from the little tin under her bed (her savings from her paid doctor visits) on the first day of her release from jail, and she left the apartment.

"Rafael Martinez. He lives on Via Primera, but you'll usually find him at a café called El Presidente…My brother Rafael, the one I told you about. If you ever do get out, he can help you. The café is called El Presidente. He works there."

Those had been Arabella's words, that day in the Valencia jail when she had been so sick, and yet she had smiled at her so sweetly. It was a long shot – Arabella was a thief and a jailbird, so she was most likely a liar, too, but Maria figured that she might as well take a chance; she had very little to lose, as it was. She would scour the streets of Madrid and find Rafael Martinez of El Presidente café.

To her unending surprised, she had done just that. He was little more than a boy – maybe nineteen, but he had a big smile, and a bear-like quality which had caused her to trust him almost immediately. Arabella had come through after all. Maria had haled a taxi, told the driver the street and the name of the place, and he had driven her right to the door. She had gone in and tentatively approached the waiter.

"I'm trying to get in touch with Rafael Martinez," she had said.

"Try no more," he had said, flashing his big white teeth. "I'm Rafael."

And by late afternoon, she had another ticket in hand, this time for the northwestern coast, for Ferrol, in Galicia, and a phone number which turned out to be that of Captain Leigh, an English captain with the Trade Winds tanker fleet. When she had phoned from the train station, which was very near the port, his voice was quite businesslike about the whole affair:

"Yes, I talked with Rafael earlier today. All is in readiness. I just request payment when you board. He told you the amount?"

"Yes, thanks," she said.

And that was all. At midnight she had climbed the ramp in the company of the somewhat rotund Captain Leigh, and soon the ship had lifted anchors and drifted into the dark, deep waters of the mid-Atlantic.

Of course, there had been the strict instructions which she supposed any stowaway should observe – don't go on deck, don't call out for any reason, don't complain about the food – but now as she sat on the edge of her bunk, she felt that she could not stand another moment. She got up, carefully unlatched the door, and put her head out in the corridor: empty. She stepped out, closed the heavy door behind her, and went softly down the corridor and up the first flight of stairs she came to.

The cool air hit her in an exuberant burst as she approached the railing. It was the joy of freedom. The sea was a huge, dark, rolling blanket, and although there was no moon tonight, the stars were sprayed across the night like diamond chips on velvet, and their reflections glittered across the swells in a thousand winks. Her heart was overwhelmed.

She heard voices, in a language she did not immediately recognize...Dutch, maybe German. They came from the bridge above her, and she shrank back into the shadows beside a couple of big crates. *Best to go back*, she thought.

> But it had been enough. A little taste of the world out there. She would last for another night; that was how it was now, step by step, little by little, one foot in front of the other one. It had been a strange and unpredictable journey so far, and it was not nearly over.

Back in her little chamber once again, she pulled out the chair and sat down at the small writing table, her only other furniture besides the bunk, which was bolted into the wall just like the ones in the Valencia jailhouse. *If only I had something to read*, she thought. Then she felt the small drawer built into the underside of the table, and she pulled it out.

Inside was a small, red paperback Bible, the same edition, precisely, as the one she had been unable to find back at her home in Valencia, the night of her husband's murder.

22

Life had almost resumed its normal course, more or less, or so it seemed to Sarah. The Negra 9 Virus was no longer the lead story on any of the network and cable news channels, as bloodlust, prurient interest, and ratings had driven these vultures to fresher roadkill. Even the trusted Pete Jones, who had frightened everyone so only a few weeks ago, had pushed the story back to a two-minute spot with vague statistics, more speculation, but very little in the way of facts regarding the numbers of women who were undergoing the experimental treatment derived through study of the bacteria found in the soft dinosaur tissue from Montana – another story they had vigorously milked. Also, the university had at last released the names of the two research scientists who had stumbled onto the dinosaur DNA connection: their names were Eastman and Curtis, and they had at once become the darlings of the media, although from the interview clips Sarah had seen they seemed to be the most reluctant of celebrities – especially Dr. Eastman, who blinked at the cameras as if he had just been awakened from a deep slumber. At least she herself was now far away from the spotlight; she thought, *I guess everyone has forgotten about "the egg woman."*

But she had to giggle, for at that precise moment, she was scrambling eggs for the boys' breakfast. In the midst of their summer break, they were sleeping late again, a Godsend really, because it gave her and Brad some quality time alone before he had to go to work. This morning, they had made good use of that time, and she smiled to think of it.

There had been offers. Despite talk of a vaccine, and despite what Sarah had said in a number of interviews, she had been solicited by three different entities – Glock-Schmidt-Klein, the Genetics Laboratory at DuPont University, and the Johnson Laboratory in Bar Harbor, Maine – concerning the harvesting of her ovaries. She had been adamant about not even considering such a course, until Brad had finally said,

"Why don't we at least hear what they have to say? We might learn something."

About a month had passed now since she had submitted to a meeting. A pair of slick marketing reps from Glock-Schmidt-Klein had come to the house to meet with them.

They'd sat in the den, and the older of the two, whose name was Richards, gave her his best undertaker's smile. "Well, Mrs. Penn, how are we feeling these days?"

"I guess we're feeling fine."

"Very good. I know you have publicly addressed the issue of egg donation, but I don't know if you've thought about the contribution you'd be making, given the current crisis."

"Oh, I've thought about it," Sarah said. "I'm just not quite ready for that. It just doesn't seem very…natural."

Richards smiled paternally, sagely. "I understand, Mrs. Penn, but I can assure you that there is nothing more natural than the impulse in any of us to do what we can for those less fortunate. Egg donation and ovarian harvesting are quite common these days."

Brad chimed in: " I didn't even know such a thing was possible."

Richards turned to him. "Oh, yes, Mr. Penn, we've had the capability to harvest a woman's ovaries and – through stimulation – cause them to produce multiple eggs since about 1983. These days it's a non-surgical procedure. This would all be contingent, of course, upon input from

Mrs. Penn's OB/GYN. But it's a very safe procedure, I assure you."

"It might be safe," Sarah said. "but what about the moral implications? Isn't this the beginning of genetic engineering or something like it? Cloning?"

"Well, no. Cloning, of course, involves the replication of cell matter. What we're speaking of here is no different from any other kind of organ donation." The other, younger man, whose name, she thought, was Burns, now spoke up:

"Now, to be frank, there are some reactionary groups out there who don't understand our purpose – the CWA, for example – "

"Yeah, I read about them," Brad said. "Concerned Women for America."

Richards chuckled. "If they were truly concerned about America, they would understand that it's critical at this time for women such as Mrs. Penn here to come forward and do what's right. You see on the news where birth rates have dwindled significantly – in some places all the way down to zero. Think about that – we're not talking about zero population *growth*. We're talking about diminishing numbers. We're talking about the future of our society, in essence."

"What about the vaccine?"

Richards smiled his superior smile once again. "There's no vaccine, Mrs. Penn. All the hullabaloo about dinosaurs – all for show. Now, what we need is citizenship, patriotism, altruism. Those are our watchwords today."

Sarah looked at Brad. He said, "I just don't know if Sarah is ready to give away such an important part of herself. I mean, we have two boys and never planned to have anymore, but…I guess we always believed that what's meant to be will be."

"Oh, I understand perfectly well, Mr. Penn. Perhaps we could just leave some information with you – nothing too technical, of course." He stood up, removed a booklet from his briefcase and handed it to Brad. He and Sarah escorted them down the hall, but at the front door, Richards turned back to them.

"And by the way, Mrs. Penn, Mr. Penn. I think you should understand that we are not talking purely about donation here. There could be a substantial sum of money involved."

She knew that Brad would not say it, on principle, so she did: "How much?"

"Oh…" Richards waved his arm. "Several million, I should think." He let the words fall upon them for a moment, and then he said. "Thank you for your time. Please get in touch with us if you're interested."

Later, when they lay in bed, it had been Brad who brought it up first: "It's really your decision, Darling. But I want you to know that I don't care about the money. It should never be about the money."

"You don't have to say that just because you think that's how I feel."

"No, I mean it," he said. He propped himself up on his elbow. "I want you to promise me that you won't give up a single egg for money."

"But Brad, I've been thinking," she said. "About the boys, about college… I want to be able to give them the best. They deserve it."

"I agree. And they'll have the best that we can give them. Not what Glock-Schmidt-Klein can give."

She took a deep breath. "All right then. We're not going to do it. We won't take a single penny."

Brad smiled at her. "In the long run, we'll be proud of ourselves. One day the boys will know we stood on principle, and that example will be the greatest gift. We haven't always made decisions that I'm proud of. We haven't always thought of others when we've done things. But we've always loved each other, and through it all, we've always tried to keep our priorities straight, even if we've failed sometimes."

She lay there thinking for a few minutes, and then she said, "This is not going to be easy."

But in truth, it had been far easier than she had imagined, that night – so far, anyway. They had heard nothing else from Richards or any of the other labs, and as the news channels and the papers had left her further and further in the rearview mirror, she had felt the pressure lifting, and she was almost content again, almost her old self.

This morning, for example, was a typical late July morning in the Penn household, and the Negra 9 Virus and ovarian harvesting and dinosaurs and all of that seemed like a dream from another life. She had just set the plates out and started down the hallway to call Alex and Ben when the doorbell rang. "That's weird," she said aloud. "Please,

God, let it not be that nut from the State Department again. He was my last unexpected caller."

But when she looked out the peephole, it was certainly *not Howell* that she saw. In fact, it seemed to be the anti-Howell – a small, petite Asian girl, in a white cotton tee shirt and khaki shorts, with a duffle bag almost as large as she was slung over one shoulder. She looked lost, as she stepped back, gazed up at the house number, and then started to turn away. Sarah opened the door.

"Yes? May I help you?" she asked.

The girl turned back. Something about her eyes was very familiar.

"Sarah Pippins?"

Suddenly it registered, and Sarah's heart leapt up. "My God," she mumbled. "Mae Ling…"

Even by 11 a.m., when they had started on their second pot of coffee, Sarah could barely believe her own eyes as she looked at Mae Ling across the breakfast counter. The boys, too, were enthralled by the presence of this extraordinary guest, and they had sat quietly watching her eat her eggs until their mother had said,

"All right, you two. Go on out to the playroom, please."

Strangely enough, Mae Ling herself seemed very much at ease, very certain that she was exactly where she was supposed to be. She chattered away in very precise English, talking about her journey, the things she had seen along the way, the people she had encountered, even the weather in the various places she had been.

"Still," she said. "There was one odd thing that happened. One night I was looking out of my hotel window in New York, and I thought I saw these two men down below, looking right at me, as if they had been watching me."

"Well," Sarah said, "it is New York, after all. Lots of perverts."

"Yes, but I could swear that I saw them again, when I went to the bus station the next day. Same car. Same haircuts."

"I wouldn't worry," Sarah said. "You're a long way from New York now."

"That's true," Mae Ling said. "I'm a long way from anywhere." As the girl looked down at her plate, Sarah thought: *That's the look I recall, that faraway expression,*

like there are things just too difficult for her to talk about.
It was there back then, too, even though we were both just
teenagers.

"Forgive my curiosity, but…well, how did you find
me? And please don't take this the wrong way, but – I
mean, you're welcome here for as long as you'd like to stay
– but why? Why did you feel you needed to seek me out?"

Mae Ling smiled. "Wait here," she said, and she
went back to the guest bedroom where Sarah had put her
bag. She returned with the copy of *National Geographic*,
though now rather ragged and torn, and she showed Sarah
the obituary for her father, John.

"Oh, gosh," Sarah said. "I never saw that. It makes
me sad."

"Don't be," Mae Ling said. "Knowing where you
were gave me hope. I'm not sure why I latched onto this.
It came to me at a time when things had been going really
badly for me, and the idea of coming to find you kept me
going. It's almost as if it were meant to happen."

Sarah sipped her coffee. "I think I know what you
mean. It's very strange…I – I've had a recurring dream
about you, Mae Ling. Do you remember when we were in

the camp, in the desert, and you and I were preparing dinner? You cut your hand."

Mae Ling held up her hand. The old scar was there.

Sarah lowered her voice almost to a whisper, in case the boys were listening in, which they probably were. "Listen. That was in my dream, the blood, running down your arm. Have you been following the news stories about that virus, Negra 9?"

Mae Ling shook her head. "I saw something about it briefly at the airport in New York. And I read it in the paper. I didn't get to watch much television back in Jining."

Sarah leaned closer across the counter. "I think my dream about you had something to do with that day. Something to do with those fossils my dad was studying."

"From the dinosaur that was killed by the meteor."

Sarah nodded. "And here's the really crazy part. I'm immune. I'm immune to Negra 9. I couldn't get it even if I wanted to. They took me to the university and ran a bunch of tests on me. And even crazier – do you remember the other scientist that was there with us? The paleontologist? Her name was Maria, and she was there with her husband, Tomas."

Mae Ling could not help physically flinching at the name. Then she stiffened in her chair, and fought back a sudden swell of nausea which rose up from deep within her. "Yes," she said. "I remember them both very well."

"She's also immune. At least, she thinks so. Last time I talked with her anyway. Now, no one really seems to know just how many women are actually carrying this thing, in the States or anyplace else. But from what I can tell, there are lots, even though they say they're working on a vaccine now, maybe even a cure. But don't you think it's a little weird? I mean, the fact that I'm immune and she's immune and the only thing we have in common is that we were both in the Gobi Desert at the same place, at the same time?"

"I guess so," Mae Ling said.

Sarah looked at her intently. "Personal question: have you seen a doctor lately?"

"No," Mae Ling said. "Not since I was with the travel agency. After I left there, things didn't really go very well for me. I guess I could have gone to the clinic, but I never did."

"Even more personal question: are you menstruating?"

Mae Ling's lips parted in surprise. "You mean right now?"

"No, I mean at all, ever?"

Mae Ling nodded.

"It's time for you to have a checkup, young lady," Sarah said, reaching for the telephone.

"She seems very sweet," Brad said, later that afternoon. He had managed to leave work a little early, and he and Sarah had gone into the den to talk things over. Mae Ling was in the shower. "But why is she here?"

Sarah shrugged her shoulders. "Fate. Why else?"

"You know I have no problem with any of this," Brad said, "but I'd just like to know how long she intends to stay. I mean, just so I'll know what to say to the neighbors."

"I don't care about the neighbors," Sarah said. "And I don't know how long she'll stay. I just know she's supposed to be here."

The telephone rang. "I'll get it," Brad said.

"Oh, it's probably my doctor. I'm trying to get her an appointment for a checkup tomorrow."

Brad went down the hallway to the kitchen. Sarah heard him pick up the phone.

"Hello?" he said. "Just a moment, please."

He appeared in the doorway again with the portable phone in his hand. "It's for you," he said. "Someone named Maria."

23

The three of them were together again, but none of them could really have said whether it was by chance or design

Maria had rented a car upon her arrival in Miami, gotten some rough directions from the rental agency, and had merely looked up the Penns' number in a phone book, once she pulled into Lake City.

"It was easy," she said. "This is nothing after you've driven in Spain."

Sarah thought that Maria looked a little tired, but otherwise, she did not seem to have aged much in ten years. She and Mae Ling had answered the door together, and they had stood in the doorway in a three-woman embrace for a good five minutes, while Brad stood back in the hallway and literally scratched his head.

"It's like old home night," he said. Alex and Ben peeped out from behind him, their faces befuddled.

At last, Sarah turned and said, "Everyone...I'd like you to meet Dr. Maria Escobar. These are the men in my life – Brad, Alex, and Ben." She fanned at her face. "I'm sorry, I'm just a little overwhelmed. Let's all go into the living room. I think we all have some catching up to do."

Brad followed them in, but he hardly knew what to think. He did not mind the commotion, and he really *didn't* care what the neighbors thought – that had been a joke – but in a strange way, it was like having *three* unfamiliar women in the house, for he had never seen Sarah so excited, so overwhelmed by her emotions. He knew that it was, in part, the associations involved – her youth, her father, their last big trip together – but it was also all mixed up somehow with the virus and the tests and all of that. He decided that his job would be to listen and to be patient, and in a little while, to think about what they would do for dinner.

After an hour or so, Ben and Alex had gone back to their rooms to play, but Brad continued to listen intently as Maria told of her satisfying life as an academic in Valencia, and the way in which it had all begun to change for her on the night of Tomas's final performance as a professional dancer. When she came to the part about the murder, Sarah leaned over and gripped her hand.

"My God," she said, "how awful! You must be still reeling from that."

"It was the beginning of a very bad time for me," Maria said.

Mae Ling took her other hand. "I'm sorry for you," she said. Only Brad noticed something in Mae Ling's voice, though, some deeper regret which suggested more than condolence.

Maria drew in her breath and looked upward. Tears welled in her eyes. "You know, sometimes, I forget that he's gone. I – haven't really had the time or space to deal with his death, on a personal level, because of everything else that has happened."

"Now you can," Sarah said. "You'll have time and space."

"It's good to be among friends at last," Maria said. "A month ago, things looked pretty hopeless." She resumed her narrative, told it all in a continuous stream, about the police investigation and the Valencia jail and about Arabella and Eduardo Sanchez (though she left out most of the intimate details concerning him), and then about Rafael Martinez and Captain Leigh and her lonely voyage aboard *The Passion*.

"Wow," Brad said, when she had finished. "What an adventure. Sounds like it should be a movie."

"No kidding," said Sarah. "And I thought *I* had had an interesting time these last few weeks."

"Oh, please, do tell me," Maria said. "You spoke briefly about it when we chatted online this past spring. I remember you asked me whether I knew anything about Mae Ling, too, and now here we are all together. It's amazing. But please, let's hear your tale."

Now it was Sarah's turn, but before she began, Brad stood up. "Excuse me, hon'," he said. "I know this part pretty well. I think I'll go outside and light the grill. I'll take some meat out of the freezer."

"Brad?" Sarah said. He turned back. "Make sure we've got plenty of wine."

"Roger that," he said.

He stood out on the deck, watching the coals going from gray to orange, and sipping on a beer, as the sun crept below the top of the wooden fence. He shook his head again. *Hard to believe, all this*, he thought. *Talk about your unexpected turns. These women…out of nowhere. Spain. China, for God's sake. Here I am, just trying to sell a little insurance in Lake City.*

He snorted, but did not laugh. *Insurance?* he thought. *No such thing.*

24

Howell sat upright in the front seat of his battered old Ford Fairlane. Cold coffee sloshed out of his metal mug and onto his plaid sport coat, but he made no attempt to reach for the napkins in the glove compartment. He was too intent on the two men in the blue Honda, who were making their fourth pass of the day down the road on which Brad and Sarah Penn lived.

"Clever bastards," he murmured. "James Bond they're not."

Still, he was relatively sure that they had to have noticed him, but this was exactly his intention. In this middle-income neighborhood, his own wax-less old paint looked more like it belonged in front of the home of some trailer-park grandmother. He was certain that the driver, the more heavyset of the two men, from what he could see, had looked right at him this time. He knew who they were well enough, and if they could muster half a brain between them, they would realize that the watchers were being watched. Still, they would probably guess he was their competition on the international market, and not an employee of the federal government. As was so often his philosophy on such assignments, he believed that the bright red plaid coat and the fluorescent shirt would mark him as being of criminal-level intelligence – in other words, as big a moron as themselves.

He had posted himself at the opposite end of the block when the two clowns from Glock-Schmidt-Klein had visited, and when he had listened back to the little recorder he had left inside the Penns' home, it was indeed the outcome he had expected. He had gotten to know Sarah a little bit during their time together in Gainesville, and had clearly seen a stubborn ethical character. Maybe she wasn't as sharp as some of the women he had worked with, but her willpower was not to be trifled with; she would not be easily swayed by the potential for monetary gain. There would have to be a different approach, he knew, one that would appeal to her sense of justice and morality. That was fine: he felt he could do that, but he had not yet gotten orders from his supervisors to make the offer. He was not surprised by this either, for folks in his department were not given to rash investments, and while government labs might not have been any better than those run by the corporations, they certainly were not any worse.

But things had gotten complicated with the arrival of the other two women. He had not expected them so soon – certainly not before the media had gotten a chance to chase down the connection to the site in the Gobi Desert, where the meteor had come down. That would be a real feeding frenzy, when it finally happened. Howell himself, once again, had not been surprised by the message when it came to him, encoded in the DVD which had reached him last week at his hotel. The movie was an old copy of a Godzilla flick – a nice touch, if a little heavy-handed. He had already pieced most of it together, anyway, especially after the Montana dinosaur DNA experiment had failed. He had thought to himself at the time, *Gotta be something more to it. Some chemical reaction between the bacteria in the tissue and something else. I was just a low-level research scientist, and even I know that.*

The "something else" was the meteor, or to be more accurate, its fragments. Their extreme heat and chemical properties had reacted with the bacteria in the dinosaur's cell tissue, and *voila*, instant immunity for anyone who came in contact with the site. Only trouble was, no one who was there had any idea yet what they would end up being immune to. The origins of Negra 9 were the real riddle. *We may not know the question,* Howell had mused, *but at least we know the answer.* It had lain in those fossilized bones and rock remains out there in the desert.

It was unclear as yet whether any other females had been in close proximity to the site, besides these three, and now here they all were in one living room. *Pretty dangerous situation, when you think about it. To think that those women in there might ultimately be the only ones to be able to bear children...unbelievable. Well, the old story has it that we started with two...Why not start over again with three?* Still, from a scientific point of view, this wasn't really feasible. Statistically, it made no sense, and despite unprecedented drops in birth rates in virtually all major population centers around the globe, there was enough variation in the data gathering to suggest that there were still plenty of women with healthy reproductive systems. It just seemed impossible to him that these could really be the only three. *Nonetheless,* he thought, *I guess I had better pay attention.*

He waited for over an hour, until darkness had fallen, and it seemed clear that the mystery men had called it a day. He started the Fairlane's engine, with a sound like the bottom falling out of a wheel barrow, cruised around the corner, and headed back to the motel.

If Sarah's story had been the most amazing because of her sudden, unsought notoriety, and if Maria's had been the most harrowing because of the sinister people with whom she had come in contact, Mae Ling's was by far the saddest. Or this was Brad's thinking, anyway, as he listened to the talk around the dinner table.

As for Mae Ling herself, she thought she had done very well at keeping her emotions in check and in leaving unsaid some of the details which she knew her companions would find rather improbable. For instance, she had not described her encounter with her father on the bridge in Jining, which she now regarded as either a real spiritual visitation (since she knew in her own soul that he must be dead) or an imaginary experience triggered by memory and desolation. But of course, Maria, who was very keen, had been the one to ask,

"But how did you know the box with the money would be there, buried behind your family's old house?"

"Well," she had stammered, "I had just abruptly remembered something my father had said about such a box, years ago, and I took a chance."

That seemed sufficient answer. Now, after the sustained intensity of Mae Ling's narrative, the women seemed excited again. The rush of conversation was also partly attributable to the happy fact that between the three of them, four bottles of wine had vanished.

"But I don't want any more negativity," Sarah was saying. "I want us all to stay together for awhile, sit down like this every night until we come up with a plan."

"What sort of plan?" Maria asked. "Why do we need a plan?"

"I'll tell you, and hear me out on this. Just let your imagination go for minute, both of you. Just forget for a moment what they want you to think – that you're small and the world is big and you don't matter that much – "

"Who are *they*?" Mae Ling asked.

"*They* are the ones who make the rules. They want you to submit your will to theirs on nearly everything that's important. The powerbrokers, the government, the corporations…including everybody who might have a stake in this Negra 9 business. And if they can't make you submit through pressure, they'll do it by trying to buy whatever you have that's important to them."

"I'm not certain what's important anymore," Maria said.

"Our immunity. Just suppose for a moment that it turns out we really are among the last women on earth capable of bearing children. That means we have a terrible responsibility."

"Or not," Maria said. "Nature dictated that dinosaurs would become extinct. Maybe the human animal has run its course as well. Or maybe God decides these things. Maybe this is the end of the story for us."

"So many maybes," Sarah said. "Maybe a meteor will hit this house within the next five minutes. I just know that ever since all of this began, I've had this overwhelming feeling that there's something I'm supposed to do, something worthwhile, something that'll help. I'm just not sure yet what it is."

"So what would you do, Sarah?" asked Mae Ling. "Supposing we are the mothers of a new world...what *could* we do?"

"Lots of stuff. I'd start with a proclamation to the world with respect to what it should strive to accomplish, and the route it should take to rebuild. I don't know, maybe we advocate for a totally new order, a global nation. It certainly hasn't worked very well the way things have gone these last couple of thousand years."

"That would mean one currency, one language," Mae Ling said.

"I vote for Spanish," Maria said.

"What's wrong with Chinese?" Mae Ling asked.

Maria frowned with mock disdain. "Chinese is impossible to learn!"

"See?" Brad said. "You all are already disagreeing. So much for your global nation."

Mae Ling continued, "But what separates Chinese from all other languages is that it's grammarless. Knowing English and Spanish, you would be amazed at Chinese, when you get into it. There are so many things it doesn't have. It doesn't have any cases, person, number, gender, degree, tense, mood, voice, infinitives, participles, gerunds, irregular verbs, and it has no articles. We have no words that are more than one syllable. Every word has only one form. I know what you're all thinking. You think this has got to be some primitive, basic language, and we'll be running around talking baby talk. But in fact, that's not true. The simpler the language, actually, the more advanced it is. Thousands of years ago, the Chinese decided to simplify their language, and after generations and generations, they changed it into a smooth-running language that could easily express ideas. Chinese is really an assembly-line language. As long as you put the words in the proper order, you can communicate effectively with less."

"Oh, fine," Maria said. "Chinese it is. We'll speak Chinese. I don't think that's going to go over so easily, but I guess we're just talking, anyway. What else should go into this proclamation, besides more wine for everyone and the Chinese language?"

"We need to make families important again," Sarah said, quite seriously. "Families are no longer as important as they used to be. Now television is important. We already know how families function, we already know the roles of the members of the family. We need to go back to the way it was intended, not the way it's presented to us on TV."

"No offense, Sarah," Mae Ling said, "but it's easy for you to say that. You've got this beautiful home with a beautiful family already. I'm really just an orphan. And Maria, she's just lost her husband. How do we even begin?"

"I will tell you this," Maria said. "You never appreciate someone – no, I take that back: you never know how essential someone is to your life until that person is gone."

"Oh, I'm not really talking about just my family," Sarah clarified. "I'm talking about an ideal. In this hypothetical family of the new world, we need to make sure that children and the elderly are the priority again, especially the elderly. In the future, it's going to be apparent as to how important children are, but the elderly are going to need looking after, too."

"That's true," Mae Ling agreed. "We used to respect the elderly a lot more than we do today. We need to go back to that."

"I think we need to teach the whole world to be thankful," Maria said. "This world is all we have. I think we've forgotten how to be thankful."

"And we need to destroy all barriers," Mae Ling added. "In America you can become or do whatever you want, for the most part. In China, you can't. Most people are stuck where they started forever, never getting the chance to improve themselves. With this new generation, we need to get rid of our old selves."

"We need healthcare for the world," Maria said. "And I'm not talking about socialized medicine. The problem is too big now for such terms. I know people say it's too hard. I don't think we try hard enough. Argentina does it, Greece does it – the whole world needs to do it."

"Then we need to get rid of the AMA," Sarah said.

"What's that?" Maria asked.

"The American Medical Association. In America, the AMA controls who gets to be doctors and who doesn't. In this country, we limit how many medical schools there are, and hence how many doctors there will be. We need more dedicated doctors. People are not willing to be doctors these days for less than four hundred thousand dollars a year. If we had twice as many doctors, their salaries would go down, and health costs would be more affordable. Insurance costs would go down."

Brad spoke up at this: "Now, I know that's just the wine talking."

"Sorry, honey. Nothing personal," Sarah said. "But it's true that better, cheaper health care would make a lot of things better. Education would be cheaper – not as many hungry or tired or angry children to deal with. Not as much violence. No more overcrowded prisons."

Maria spoke up. "I don't know about America," she said, "but Spain must completely reform its prison system. We must start building a prison system that believes in rehabilitation rather than strictly punishment."

"And one last thing," Sarah said. "Men and women need to be paid equally for the same work. No exceptions. But if I choose to be a stay-at-home mom, then why shouldn't I at least get some respect for all the work involved in that?"

"What do you mean?" Brad complained. "*I* know how much work you do!"

"Oh, Brad, I'm not talking about you. I just mean in society in general."

"Wait a minute," Mae Ling said, setting down her wine glass. "You've left out superconductivity at room temperature."

"What?"

"You know, like the magnet train in Japan. It costs almost nothing to transport people at super high speed with it, but it all revolves around bringing large amounts of electricity down the line, and doing that cheaply requires superconductivity at room temperature."

They all gazed at her in bewilderment. Then Brad said, "Speaking of room temperature, would anyone like some more wine before I go to bed?"

25

Howell could barely believe what he had just seen. Granted, he had been rather surprised to see the Chinese girl come out of the house at such an early hour, but still, he should have known. Jetlag. Couldn't sleep. That much was understandable.

Then the new blue Honda with the two idiots aboard came cruising around the corner, but he still had not been alarmed. And when they slowed and rolled down their window to talk to her, even then, he fully expected her either to keep walking or to simply go back to the house. Smart kid, he knew.

But she did neither of those things. To his disbelief, she went over, leaned down, spoke with them, and then she got into the car. She got into the frigging car!

He rubbed his eyes. They were gone, moving pretty quickly. He cranked up the Fairlane, and it growled back to life. *Damn it*, he thought. *I tried to tell them I'm not trained for this kind of shit. Who do they think I am, anyway, James Bond?*

An elderly woman in a vintage red Mustang backed out of her driveway in front of him and then proceeded to edge along at stroller speed. Oh, my God, can you believe it? Howell thought. By the time he came up to the stop sign at the end of the street – a fairly busy intersection, buzzing with early-morning commuters, it was too late.

The blue car had squeezed out into the relentless flow and disappeared.

The three women had stayed up until nearly two a.m., hashing over their ideas for a new world order. Sarah had even taken out a notepad and begun writing things down, shouting, "Yes! Yes! Right!" when either Maria or Mae Ling came up with a new tenet, a new item to add to their proclamation.

Finally, it was Maria who had looked up at the clock. "*Dios Mio*," she said. "In Spain, it's eight in the morning. Time for coffee."

"That's nothing," Mae Ling said. "In China, it's Friday."

Sarah had snapped the notepad shut. "Well, in Lake City it's bedtime. Come on, you two. Might as well start getting adjusted."

They had said their goodnights, hugged one another again, expressed their pleasure and excitement at their unexpected reunion.

Maria slept soundly, almost as soon as she lay down. She still felt the motion of the tanker's hull under her, but by the time the first wave had rolled beneath, she was far gone, drifting in that sweet, dreamless sleep which helps to re-knit mind and soul.

Sarah, still listing badly to her left, had just enough strength to brush her teeth, remove all of her clothes, and then fall into the bed next to Brad. To her surprise, he was wide awake.

"Whassa matter?" she mumbled.

"Um, I don't know. Somebody was making a lot of noise out there. Can't imagine."

"Sorry," she said.

"It's all right," he said. "Special occasion. I'm gonna be pretty limp at work, though. Maybe I can come home for a nap at lunch."

Her hand wandered down along his body. "That's funny," she said. "You don't seem all that limp right now."

"Hmm," he said. "What do you know about that?"

"Oh, I know all about this," she said.

"But you're too sleepy for anything," he said.

"Who needs sleep?" she asked, rousing herself. "I don't need sleep. I may never feel like sleeping again."

But a few minutes later, when they were fully into that mutual rhythm they knew so well and which was theirs alone and apart from the rest of the world, she remembered something: she had not taken her pill, tonight or last night.

Oh, well, the egg woman thought. *It's just once.*

Mae Ling, however, was restless. Even though she was smallest in stature of the three, her body was younger and stronger and more prone to recovery. She had a slight headache, but other than that, the effects of the wine were nearly gone by the time a pale light snuck in at the bottom of the blinds in her room.

She rose, put her khaki shorts back on, along with her t-shirt and sneakers, and as an afterthought, she dug in her duffel bag to find the bone-handled knife she had bought in the pawn shop in New York, and she slipped it into her back pocket. Then she padded down the hallway softly so as not to awaken anybody, and she slipped out the front door for an early-morning walk.

Even at this hour, the humid Florida air washed over her like a warm bath. Those days when she had wandered the streets of Jining, like a ghost, like a shell of a human being, seemed long ago. She saw now that through all of it she had been falling, falling, and that day when she stood on the bridge, she had been about to make her final descent when her father – or his spirit – had appeared to her. He had saved her life, and since then she had felt his presence many times. She felt it now, as she pulled the door to and strode out to meet the dawn. *Be ready*, his voice said.

She was. Somehow, she was not even frightened when the blue Honda with New York plates pulled alongside her. The car itself was dirty now, obviously from the many miles it had covered, but the two men looked chipper, even friendly.

"Hi," the one in the passenger seat said.

"Hi," she said.

"I know you, don't I?" he asked.

"I don't think so." She stopped in the road and turned to face them.

"No, I do. Perhaps you don't remember. We met in New York. We've been trying very hard to catch up to you."

"Oh?" she said. "What are you doing here?"

"I have a very important message for you. It's from your father."

She went over to the car's window and leaned over. "My father?"

"Yes. I'm sorry." He smiled. "I know this must be unnerving for you."

"I'm not unnerved," she said. "What's the message?"

"That's the only problem," the man said. "My supervisors won't let me tell you. They want to meet with you. My colleague here and I are with the U.S. military." He held up a picture ID in a plastic folder. "Your father has been trying to reach you from his base in China."

"My father is…dead," she said.

"Oh, I assure you, Mae Ling, he's very much alive. And he has sent a letter for you, but for international security reasons, you'll have to come with us in order to sign for it. Routine procedure. It's a very tense situation in the world right now, you know."

"Where's the letter?"

"Tyndall Air Force Base. It's not terribly far from here."

She hesitated and looked back at the Penn house. "I'll have to let my friends know where I'm going."

He smiled. "I'm sure they're all still asleep. You can use my cell phone to call them later. We'll have you back by mid-afternoon. Promise."

She paused. And suddenly, as if prompted by some irresistible impulse, she opened the back door of the car and got in.

Sarah awakened around 8:15, when Brad came in to kiss her goodbye. He was still crunching on some cereal and fumbling with his tie.

"Have a good day," she mumbled. "Think you'll be home for lunch?"

"I doubt it," he said. "Tons of paperwork. But maybe I can sneak out a little early again."

"Mm," she said. "By the way, last night was great."

"I've heard that one before," he said. "Besides, it was morning when you came to bed."

"Whatever, honey."

She lay there for a few more minutes after he was gone, and then she forced herself to get up. The boys would be going full tilt soon. When she stood, the room took a sharp swoop, and she held onto the bedpost. "Why – why did I do that?" she asked aloud. "I must really hate my head."

She put on her bathrobe, brushed her teeth, and then stumbled out to the kitchen, drawn by the promising hiss of the coffee pot. When she had poured herself a cup and started back down the hall for a shower, she noticed that the door to the room she had put Mae Ling in was ajar. *That's weird.* She peeped in: the bed was made, and her guest's suitcase was neatly tucked under it. She had hung some clothes up in the closet, and had set out a few things on top of the chest of drawers: a hair band, brush, deodorant – and she took particular note of a plastic baggie containing three tampons. But there was no Mae Ling.

She went to the front door, stepped out, and looked up and down the street. The air was dank and heavy, and the sun was firing it all in a glaze like hot wax. *I don't feel good about this*, Sarah thought. She went back in and woke up Maria.

"Ooh," Maria groaned. "My head."

"I know," Sarah said. "It was the merlot. Listen, though – Mae Ling is not here. Her things are in the room, but...I mean, I didn't hear her go out, so I think she's been gone for quite some time."

"Probably just went for a walk," Maria said. "Anyway, she's a big girl."

"I guess you're right. But if she's not back by eleven, I'm going to call someone. Would you care for some coffee?'

"God, yes," Maria moaned. "I feel horrible. It's my stomach, too. I know we had a little too much, but wine doesn't usually treat me *this* poorly."

"I'll get the coffee."

Mae Ling had been taken to one of those undistinguished strip malls which infest American cities like square fungi, made of synthetic blocks of some color definitely not found in nature. A few straggly shrubs clung to life in a patch of gray dirt that passed for a courtyard. For some reason, the complex was called Atlantic Plaza, even though they were not very near the Atlantic Ocean. There were a few businesses, she noted – Florida Title Company, Wickendom Real Estate, Empire Auto Insurance

– but mostly they were nondescript offices with blank signs on their beige doors.

Her two escorts, who had spoken little to her and even less to each other during the drive, unlocked one of the doors and led her in. There was a metal desk, a couple of plastic chairs, one interior door, but no windows.

"This doesn't look much like an air force base," she said.

"Top security location," the heavier man said. "Just have a seat there, and one of our officers will bring out your father's letter." And the two of them left, bolting the door from the outside.

She sat in the plastic chair, thinking: *I suppose he could have written the letter, if there is one, before…before anything happened to him. I'm certain that he's passed on. He has, and Mother has. But how could he have gotten it out, and how could it have found me here? No, none of this makes any sense. What could they possibly want with me?* She shut her eyes and leaned her head back. It was not good to sit still for too long.

God will protect you.

"What?" she couldn't tell if that voice had been in her own mind or if she someone had actually said it. "What did you say?"

"I said hello, Mae Ling."

The voice was deadly in its familiarity –the accent was Spanish. She snapped her head forward. A man had entered the room and was standing behind the desk, though she had not heard him come in. But when she saw him, she knew him instantaneously.

"You," she said. It was Tomas Escobar. The moustache was gone, the haircut
very short, but there was no mistaking.

"You remember me then," he said.

She stared at him, feeling the blood dropping through her face. "I have never forgotten you, even for one day," she said.

He smiled. "I certainly hope we're not harboring any hard feelings. It was years ago when we saw one another last. We were both very young."

"*I* was very young," she said.

He cleared his throat. "Let's just say that what happened must have happened for a reason. Even if it was just a misunderstanding, perhaps something good came about because of it. Maybe we didn't even really know what we were doing. That is how relationships go, you see."

"There was no relationship," she said. "You knew what you were doing, but I didn't. But I do now. I know what happened in the tent that day. And I have not let a single day pass without remembering to despise you."

The smile drifted from his face. "Be that as it may, I have brought you here in order to speak with you about something very important, Mae Ling."

"They told me this was military business. My father…"

"Para-military," he said. "But that is beside the point. I'm very sorry to say that the letter from your father was a made-up story. It was crucial that you come here today. You see, you have a very great gift, and I am prepared to make you a wonderful offer if only you'll share this gift."

"What gift could I possibly have?"

"Why, it's your ability to have children, to become a mother. I'm sure you know that there are many places around the world today which are suffering very dire circumstances. A terrible disease has caused a great blight…"

"You don't need to address me as if I were an ignoramus," she said.

"I'm sorry. Because of the Negra 9 virus, there is great fear that an entire generation of the human family will be lost, and believe me, the situation is truly much worse than our governments or the media are willing to admit at present. Women who are immune – women whose ovaries are functional – are highly prized on the global market. So, I'm prepared to offer you a substantial sum of money, Mae Ling, if you will allow the company I represent to extract your ovaries, or 'harvest' them, as they say, for the purpose of producing fertile human eggs. The fact is, you, Mae Ling, can contribute to a secure future for us all."

She gaped at him in disbelief. "You're offering…"

"Ten million dollars," he said. "Negotiable."

She leaned forward and put her head in her hands. "This has got to be a bad dream," she said.

"No dream," Tomas said. "Think of all the good you can do with such money, Mae Ling. You could return to China, find your sister, build an orphanage… Or stay here in America, go to college, become a doctor. The future will be at your command, you'll have something the rest of us all long for: control over your own destiny."

She raised her head, the heat and the tears suddenly springing into her eyes. "After everything, after what you did to me... after, after... Why are you not dead? Maria told us you were dead."

"Maria? I'm afraid that's not possible. My wife is in a jail cell in Valencia. I'm sure she hasn't told you anything of the sort."

"You're wrong. She's here. She's in Lake City, at Sarah's house."

She could see that Tomas was genuinely upset by this. "Impossible," he said. "Don't play a game with me."

"You're too stupid to know. Your two thugs were too stupid even to realize it. Stupid, stupid."

He came around to the front of the desk threateningly. "Let me tell you something," he said. "I didn't arrive at this point in my life by being stupid. You don't know what I have accomplished just in the last year. Why, I have brokered deals among some of the most powerful people in the world. You are incidental to any of this..." He was working himself into a frenzy, but now he paused, seemed to collect himself.

"How do you know that I'm immune to the virus?" she asked.

"Ah. You might as well know." He smiled again, basking in his superior knowledge. The news networks will break the story any day now. The key was the fossil site in the Gobi desert, the one where you and I first met. The collision caused a chemical reaction between a bacteria in the dinosaur's tissue and the meteor fragments. The fact that I was actually once at the site myself increases my credibility, wouldn't you think? Anyway, the answer to the disease's riddle was imbedded in those old bones and rocks."

"Then why don't you just go and buy the bones and rocks?"

"Excellent idea, Mae Ling, but unfortunately someone has already taken them. They have all disappeared. We think the Chinese government has them. That leaves us with you."

"And two others."

"Yes, well, so far Sarah Penn has been somewhat stubborn, but I think she might ultimately see the light. She has a good soul, and she'll finally do the right thing. As for Maria, it was unfortunate, what happened to her, but one day she will understand the necessity for it. I needed utter freedom in order to start my second career, and as long as she is in custody, then I know exactly where she is. She will keep for a while, and believe me, then she and I will be together again. 'Till death do us part,' eh? Not dead, then not truly parted."

Mae Ling stood up. "You might as well unlock that door," she said. "You're offer is no good. I have the Negra 9 virus. My ovaries are infected. They're useless to you."

He took a step toward her and spoke through clenched teeth: "I told you not to play games with me."

"I'm not. It's true. I stopped menstruating months ago."

His hand shot out and gripped her jaw in a cold vice. "Is that so? We'll have to have one of our doctors have a look at you."

"Let me out," she said, and she began to resist, grabbing his wrist and trying to twist it, kicking at his knees with her sneakers.

Tomas laughed. "A little stronger than you used to be," he said. "But still just a little girl…" With his other hand, he tore the front of her t-shirt from the collar down, exposing her bra and torso. Then he reached behind her head and knotted his fingers in her black hair.

With her first strike, the knife went into his armpit, all the way up past the hilt, and she had to pull it back quickly again in order not to let go of it, as he brought his arm down reflexively. Then he lifted it again and looked in disbelief at the hole in his shirt's underarm and the blood which had already begun to run in a steady trickle down his side. He looked at her, mouth open, eyes wide.

"What *is* that? What do you have…"

His words were clipped mid-sentence as the second strike found its mark just below his Adam's apple, severing his windpipe. She twisted it quickly, before pulling it out again. A dark red line ran down her arm and curled around her elbow as she held the knife aloft for a moment. He put his hand to his throat and sat back heavily on the desk, still looking at her in astonishment.

The last one was a broad slash across his lower abdomen, and again, the four-inch blade did its work, going in all the way past the hilt and moving in a clean line from one hip to the other. She could feel the cloth of his shirt, his skin, his muscle, and the soft intestines all tearing with a single strong motion. With no bone to block its passage, it was like passing her hand through water, and she slashed back again in the opposite direction just to make sure. Then she stepped back.

Both of his arms had now fallen to his sides, and he looked at her sadly, and his lips moved; he was trying to say something, but with the effort a single red bubble of blood slipped from the hole in his throat. He could only sit there on the edge of the metal desk.

There was a noise. She didn't know how long she had been hearing it, but someone was pounding on the heavy beige door. She moved sideways, but Tomas's eyes continued to stare at the spot where she had been standing.

In a trance, she went to the door, as the pounding increased in fierceness. "Who is it?" she shouted.

"Open up!" a voice cried.

She looked down at the bolt, and then carefully she reached out and turned it, and the door swung inward.

A man in a plaid jacket and a bright yellow shirt was standing there. His eyes traveled from her face down to the bone-handled knife which was still in her hand and back to her face again.

"Mae Ling?" he said.

She nodded. "Yes, I'm Mae Ling."

26

Two weeks had passed since the arrival of Sarah's houseguests, and the excitement had not abated. If anything, it had intensified, and even the boys were affected by the general feeling of ongoing festivities. Indeed, each day had been like a feast, each night like a carnival.

There had been plenty of wine, except for Maria, who after several mornings of nausea and headaches had realized that she was not hung over after all, but pregnant. When she and the other two women had looked together at the e.p.t. strip as it changed colors, it was Sarah who said, "Uh-huh. I knew there was something more to this thing you had with that lawyer than just a professional relationship."

"Can't put anything over on you, I guess," Maria said. "Now get out of the way, please. I've already asked you not to stand between me and that toilet."

Mae Ling, especially, had seemed much happier since the day of her very long walk. She had indeed gone out early in the morning, as Sarah had guessed, but she had phoned around 10:30 to say that she would be out for the rest of the day but would be back for dinner ("Just doing some exploring," or so she had explained). In any case, after that day, she had loosened up considerably, laughing more than any of them, embracing anyone near her at the slightest provocation, beaming, dancing, glorying in her new freedoms.

Brad, Alex, and Ben watched it all in a kind of bemused curiosity, but they had certainly been infected, too, by the overall atmosphere of jollity. Brad, in particular, reveled in his wife's happiness, but he knew it was not just the presence of her two old friends, but also had much to do with the latest news. Once the Center for Disease Control's research team had understood the importance of the Gobi Desert meteor site, and the nature of the chemical chains still present in those dinosaur fossils and meteor rocks, a Chinese professor had come forward with samples he'd remembered he had stored in his basement a few years earlier.

They had seen him on television, holding two of the rocks and grinning, an ancient man with eyes which were wells of kindness and contentment. One could see the boy in those eyes.

"Oh, that's sweet," Sarah had said. Then she had glanced at her two friends and said, "I guess they won't need our help after all, ladies."

"No," Brad agreed. "But it was a wild ride, wasn't it?"

Three days later, at the airport, they all waited by the gate, the two boys hopping about and the adults standing in a circle together. Brad said to Sarah, "Now, where is it you all are going again?"

"Very funny," she said.

"Seriously," he said. "I don't understand. Why are you going back to the Gobi Desert? There's nothing there anymore, no bones, no fossils. All gone, excavated, kaput."

Maria broke in: "Sometimes you go someplace not really knowing what you'll find, or what you'll bring back. We thought we found some old bones and rocks the first time, but we really ended up with was each other. Who knows what we'll find this time?"

"Besides," Sarah said, "it's a reunion, of sorts. People always go back for reunions."

"Okay," he said. "I thought that's what we've been having for the past three weeks, but…whatever. If you want to go, go."

Mae Lin grinned. "What a good sport," she said.

"Isn't he?" Maria said. "You've really trained him well, Sarah. He's learned a thing or two. I only wish that my Tomas were here to see *me* off as well. I know he would have been as good about it as you are, Brad."

"I know he would have, Maria," Sarah said.

Mae Ling said nothing, but rubbed her friend's back, and smiled her secret smile.

The intercom rattled: it was time to board the plane.

Brad, Alex, and Ben stood waving as the women walked up the ramp, even though none of the three had yet looked back, so absorbed were they in their never-ending conversation. "I guess they're just too excited," Brad said.

Then, at the very last instant, just before the door shut and they had disappeared from view, his wife turned back, saw him, and blew him a kiss.

Epilogue

With his cereal bowl on his lap, the boy, whose name was Kevin, climbed into the big puffy chair. When his head touched the back of it, the screen swung down in front of him, and the lovely woman appeared, as she always did. She said:

"Good morning, Kevin. How are you this morning?"

"I'm fine," he said.

"Very good. Can you tell me the time and date?"

He looked at the tip of his right index finger, and the little screen opened like an eyelid. "It's Tuesday, September five," he said. "8:03 a.m. Year 2601."

"Good. How would you like to begin today? We didn't finish our physics lesson yesterday. Or we could start with mythology."

"Um...mythology sounds good."

"Very well. I'll begin the narration if you'll activate the image scanner."

He put his head back against the seat again, and immediately a few of his dream figures appeared before him in hologram form, left over from the previous night's brain activity – there was his father, waving at him from a train, and there was a big dog, too, licking an ice cream cone.

"All right, Kevin. Please clear your mental screens now."

As he had been taught to do, he was able to create a sense of blank space in the air before him, and then she said, "Good. Now, if you'll recall, yesterday we dealt with the chapter concerning the Third Pestilence. Do you remember how that was resolved?"

Kevin shut his eyes for a moment. "Sure. Let me see…the Third Pestilence… Oh, yes. The Third Pestilence was solved when the Three Queens of the Old World shot their golden arrows over the earth, after the Race of Machines had failed once again." He opened his eyes.

"Correct," his teacher said. Now, let us review the myth of the Three Queens of the Old World. First, there was the Fair-haired Queen. Her name was…"

There was a pause, and Kevin said, "Sarah," and when he said the name, the blank hologram screen became a green sea, and he saw the queen with the golden hair riding on a great ship.

"Correct. Long ago, Sarah sailed over that part of the Old World we called the Great Barrier Reef, near the ancient continent of Australia. When she pulled her solid gold arrow out of its quiver, she saw that the arrow was inscribed: 'Let the world know God with all their heart, and let the world come to God with all that they are.' She set her arrow on the great bow, and she drew the string back with all her might. She said those words again to herself, and let fly the arrow, into the sky, and when it was almost beyond sight, it turned, blazing brightly in the sun. Then it streaked toward the water, entering the sea and at last striking the bottom, never to be seen again."

As his teacher's voice described these events, Kevin watched the images produced within his own mind and projected before him – the Golden Queen was beautiful, and looked a good deal like his own mother.

"Next, the Queen with the Heart of Fire went to the great river we once called the Nile. She took her son with her. And her name was…"

"Maria."

"That's correct. With her son, this queen sat upon
the riverbank, and she produced a golden arrow, just as
Queen Sarah had done. Inscribed on it were the words 'Let
the world change what they value, and let the world learn
what is prestigious before God.' Then she set the arrow
upon her bow's string, looked into her son's eyes, and
pulled the arrow back and released it. It pierced the sky
and traveled the length of the river – the longest river in the
world – and then disappeared forever."

The two figures in the hologram enacted the story,
just as his teacher told it.

"Finally, the Queen With the Sad Eyes sat by
herself on a beach – a beach so white it would hurt our eyes
to see it. This queen was named…"

"Mae Ling," Kevin trumpeted.

"Right again," his teacher said. "Mae Ling, the
Sad-eyed Queen, reached down for her arrow, which was
lying on the beach beside her. But it was very hot to her
touch. She retrieved a cupful of water from the ocean and
poured it onto the arrow, to cool it down. She took the
golden arrow in hand and read the inscription on it: 'A
noble character is worth more than rubies.' She pulled the
bow back with all her might, but a demon suddenly

287

appeared before her, and snatched her bow from her, breaking it in half.

The Sad-eyed Queen wept all that day, lamenting the loss of her bow and believing she had failed in God's eyes. Then, as evening drew on, she saw that the tide had left her a new bow, glittering in the sand. She picked it up, fitted her arrow, and aiming toward the heavens, she let go."

Kevin's brain projected the image – the arrow climbed to the outer edge of the hologram and became blurred.

"The arrow flew well past the waves, and even beyond the sun, farther, farther, until it pierced the water's breast without a splash or a sound, and it was lost forever at the bottom of the ocean."

The Beginning